SPURS
and
SPARKS

Books by Jody Hedlund

Healing Springs Ranch
Spurs and Sparks
Broncos and Ballads

High Country Ranch
Waiting for the Rancher
Willing to Wed the Rancher
A Wife for the Rancher
Wrangling the Wandering Rancher
Wishing for the Rancher's Love

Colorado Cowgirls
Committing to the Cowgirl
Cherishing the Cowgirl
Convincing the Cowgirl
Captivated by the Cowgirl
Claiming the Cowgirl: A Novella

Colorado Cowboys
A Cowboy for Keeps
The Heart of a Cowboy
To Tame a Cowboy
Falling for the Cowgirl
The Last Chance Cowboy

A Shanahan Match
Calling on the Matchmaker

Saved by the Matchmaker
A Wager with the Matchmaker

Bride Ships: New Voyages
Finally His Bride
His Treasured Bride
His Perfect Bride
His Unforgettable Bride

Bride Ships Series
A Reluctant Bride
The Runaway Bride
A Bride of Convenience
Almost a Bride

Orphan Train Series
An Awakened Heart: A Novella
With You Always
Together Forever
Searching for You

Beacons of Hope Series
Out of the Storm: A Novella
Love Unexpected
Hearts Made Whole
Undaunted Hope
Forever Safe
Never Forget

Evermore

Foremost

Hereafter

Noble Knights Series

The Vow: Prequel Novella

An Uncertain Choice

A Daring Sacrifice

For Love & Honor

A Loyal Heart

A Worthy Rebel

Waters of Time Series

Come Back to Me

Never Leave Me

Stay With Me

Wait for Me

A HEALING SPRINGS RANCH NOVEL

SPURS
and
SPARKS

JODY HEDLUND

NORTHERN LIGHTS PRESS

Spurs and Sparks
Northern Lights Press
© 2025 by Jody Hedlund
Jody Hedlund Print Edition
ISBN 979-8-9896277-5-2

Jody Hedlund www.jodyhedlund.com

Cover Design by RoseannaWhiteDesigns.com

1

"Dad, why don't you have yourself a woman?"

Tyler McQuaid, in the middle of casting his fishing line, slipped on the wet stones beneath his waders. He threw out both hands and tried to steady himself, but the rushing river was too strong. In the next instant, he found himself falling backward into the mountain runoff, still icy cold for May. He landed with a splash, his fly rod falling from his grip into the Badger River.

A dozen paces ahead in the shallow water, Wyatt glanced over his shoulder, his innocent seven-year-old eyes widening. "What's wrong?"

Sitting waist-deep in the river, Tyler could only stare at his son, a miniature version of himself with a stocky frame, dark-brown hair, deep-set eyes, and a strong, square jawline. The kid was wearing a black Stetson and was outfitted in his own waders and flannel shirt, just like Tyler's.

"Dad?" Wyatt persisted as he swiped up the pole floating past him.

"Your question surprised me a little. That's all."

Perched on a log a short distance from the river, Anson guffawed obnoxiously. The old cowboy-turned-nanny paused in his whittling of mushroom replicas to lift his brows at Tyler, his eyes saying everything—that Wyatt's question hadn't surprised him just *a little*. No, it had surprised him so much that it had knocked him off his feet.

Anson's long gray hair was slicked back and covered with a battered and sweat-stained cowboy hat that was probably as old as the cowboy himself. He was wiry and short and muscular, still fit from his days as a horse jockey.

As Tyler began to push up from the river, he glared at the man. "I don't need any of your smart-aleck remarks tonight."

Anson's gap-toothed smile wrinkled his leathery face. "I didn't say anything."

"I asked the question, Dad." Wyatt started wading upriver, his own child-sized fly-fishing pole in one hand and Tyler's much longer rod in the other.

The slant of the sun coming off the western mountain range turned the water droplets into diamonds. The sunlight also glinted on the fir trees mingling with the aspens that were bright with new leaves and rustling in the mountain breeze. It was the most peaceful and most beautiful time of the day in the high country of Colorado.

Tyler sighed. Too bad they couldn't ever just fish in silence.

But no. Wyatt usually had something to say. "At school today, Levi wanted to know why you don't have a woman."

"Why are you guys talking about a subject like that?" Water droplets rolled down Tyler's water-resistant pants and boots, although he already could feel the chill and dampness of the water against his skin.

"He heard his mom talking about you and saying it was past time for you to have a woman."

Tyler frowned. Nettie needed to be more careful what she was talking about around her son. Neither Levi nor Wyatt was old enough to understand anything about relationships, particularly about divorce. Wyatt had been only two when Stephanie left. He'd never known what it was like to have a mother around.

So why the curiosity now?

"Thirty-two's not all that old."

"It's ancient, Dad."

Anson chortled outright, the cackling rising above the rustling river and echoing in the stillness of the evening.

Tyler glared again at the cowboy nanny who'd been working for the family since Tyler was a boy. "I'm not as ancient as Anson."

"Anson says he has all kinds of women."

"Oh really?" Tyler cocked a brow at the old man.

Anson bent his head and studied his mushroom intently, smoothing away shavings and rubbing at it as if it were the most important thing in the world.

"Oh, that's right." Tyler didn't let up. "Anson has all those girlfriends at his Saturday night senior bingo club."

Anson spit on his thumb and then wiped a spot on the mushroom. "At least I got some pretty ladies who like me. That's more than I can say for you."

"I think Levi's mom likes Dad." Wyatt just shrugged. "At least, that's what Levi said."

Tyler shook his head as he neared Wyatt. "We're doing all right without a woman, aren't we?"

Wyatt handed him the wayward pole, his expression serious. "Why don't you want a woman? It might be real nice to have one around."

"We have Grandma and Aunt Emberly."

This time Anson snorted, and it was loud enough to rival a moose about to charge.

"Besides," Tyler continued without giving Wyatt a chance to say that Grandma and Aunt Emberly didn't count. "I'm busy with the ranch. You know that."

He'd taken over managing their luxury ranch resort from his dad the year he'd graduated from the University of Colorado, and he'd been in charge ever since. Ten years, to be exact.

Of course, his dad had continued to help in a public-relations role, which suited his personality better than the everyday management of the ranch's operations.

"You've got the ranch running great." Wyatt spoke with a seriousness that a child of seven shouldn't have. "Maybe you should focus on something else now. Like getting me a mom."

Tyler opened his mouth to respond, but nothing came out. What could he say anyway? Wyatt already had a mom, but maybe the boy wasn't satisfied with the once- or twice-a-year visits with Stephanie and was beginning to want more than just a dad provided.

"Listen, Wyatt—" At the buzz of his phone, he fished it out of his back pocket to see his mom's name and profile filling the screen. He tapped open the call. "Hi, Mom."

"Tyler." His mom's voice was breathless and strained.

"What's up?" With the dry fly missing from his line, Tyler began to slosh toward his tacklebox sitting on the river's edge near Anson.

"It's your dad."

Stepping out onto the rocky embankment, Tyler came to an immediate halt.

"He's having back pain again," his mom rushed. "It's so bad that he fell and can't get up."

Dad had been having bouts of back pain recently, and Tyler had tried to make him take it easy. Of course, Dad was a stubborn and determined McQuaid and never rested.

"Where are you?"

"We're at the house."

"Don't try to lift him. I'll be right there."

"He's throwing up, Ty." Mom's voice wavered with worry. "And he's complaining of stomach pain now too."

"This sounds more serious than just a strained back."

"I think so too."

Tyler's mind whirred. He had to come up with a solution and manage the situation. Fast. "We need to take him in to the ER."

"That's what I was thinking. I've already asked Kade to get the helicopter ready."

In Park County, the ranch wasn't near an emergency room. For severe situations, they almost always used the helicopter and flew to Colorado Springs, which was only about sixty miles away. His youngest brother, Kade, had a pilot's license and was the one they relied on to get them where they needed to go.

"I'm worried, Ty," his mom whispered, probably trying to keep Dad from hearing her.

"It'll be fine." At least, Tyler hoped it would be. "Hold tight, and I'll be there in a few minutes."

He ended the call and then shot a quick call to Kade. As he finished and stuffed his phone into his pocket, Anson was at his side, his forehead furrowed.

"Something wrong with T.W.?"

"More back pain." All the employees at Healing Springs Ranch loved his dad, especially the old-timers like Anson.

Anson's scowl deepened. Since he lived at the main house, he'd heard Dad's recent complaints about his back. Just yesterday, Dad had tried to put on his cowboy boots and had nearly buckled over with a spasm.

They should have taken Dad to the doctor then. When they'd suggested it, Dad had claimed he was okay.

They'd believed him. Because Dad had always been as healthy as a horse—active and alert, energetic and enthusiastic, calling Tyler with new ideas and plans, his vision for the ranch still alive and abounding, even though he'd pulled back to give Tyler the final say on everything.

"C'mon, Wyatt. Time to go." He regretted that he had to cut short their Friday activity night, but there wasn't even time to gather up their fly-fishing gear. He'd send one of the employees out to retrieve everything later. For now, he needed to get to Dad and figure out what was going on.

Tyler climbed to the UTV on the trail above the river. He slid into the driver's seat and started up the vehicle. A moment later, Wyatt and Anson were scrambling into the back seats. Tyler waited for them to buckle in, then he gunned the small four-wheeled off-road vehicle down the trail.

He wound his way along the paths behind the largest and most elaborate of the private luxury cabins. All of them were styled in Western themes and furnished with only the best furniture and appliances. They had full-sized kitchens, king suites, spacious lofts, sitting areas with wood-burning fireplaces, private patios with hot tubs, and more.

The smaller cabins were no less lavish and were beautifully decorated with screened-in porches that faced the river. Although equipped with kitchenettes, most of the guests took their meals in the Cliffside Dining Room in the lodge, where the chef prepared daily farm-to-table meals that everyone raved about. The ranch also had a smaller dining area in Brook Barn that offered simpler fare and snacks.

As Tyler reached the main pathway, he jerked to a stop while a young couple meandered past, walking hand in hand, likely staying in one of their honeymoon cabins, which were a Forbes Travel Guide five-star recommendation.

As soon as he started forward, he veered onto the uphill lane that led to his family's home. The main house was set away from the resort to allow for privacy but was still close enough that they could be involved in any issues and needs that might arise.

At the sound of the chopper engine and wings roaring to life at the landing pad on a plateau above the house,

Tyler released a pent-up breath. Kade was ready to go, probably already had the stretcher at the house.

As Tyler flew up the final incline, the modern two-story log home came into view on the rise. With a prominent peaked prow at the center and windows from floor to ceiling, the great room faced the west so that viewing sunsets was almost a nightly occasion.

On each side of the peak, the house sprawled out with additional tall windows. A large deck on the main level of the house contained a hot tub and patio furniture, while a porch swing and hammock were positioned on the grassy knoll underneath.

Tyler steered the UTV around the driveway that led to the back of the house, which had a cozy but small porch with rustic-looking rocking chairs. The ranch's interior decorator had styled their home both inside and out with Western-themed decorations like all the other homes on the ranch, and it was just as interesting and unique.

The main house had six bedrooms, which was plenty big enough for him and each of his four siblings to have had their own rooms while growing up. Now only he and Wyatt lived there with Mom and Dad.

As head wrangler, Kade preferred bunking with the other ranch hands in one of the apartments over the main barn. His sister Emberly, who was the events manager, stayed in one of the employee cottages near the main lodge. Of course, Brock was busy with his career as a country music singer, and ever since Dustin had left his position as an elite army ranger, he'd put his skills to use as a bodyguard for an executive protection company and traveled all over the world for his work.

Yes indeed, he and Wyatt and Mom and Dad had more than enough space. Sometimes too much.

Tyler halted the UTV and jumped out. He didn't wait for Wyatt or Anson—was grateful in this instant to know that Anson was taking care of the boy. Instead, Tyler bolted into the house and to his parents' bedroom.

"Hey," he called, stepping into the spacious room.

Mom stepped out of the master bathroom, tears streaking her face.

With her wavy red hair pulled back into a clip, she appeared younger than her fifty-five years and was still as beautiful as in the pictures on the wall from when she'd been crowned Miss Colorado years earlier.

"How is he?"

"Oh Tyler, I'm so worried. He's in terrible pain and can't stop moaning."

Tyler sidled past her into the bathroom with its clean white interior, jacuzzi tub, and walk-in shower. It was more spacious than most bathrooms, with two walk-in closets, a dressing table, and a chaise. He halted at the sight of his brawny dad writhing on the ground, clutching his stomach and moaning.

Tyler's chest tightening, he dropped to his knees beside the man who had been not only his mentor and friend but also the rock who'd held him up through some really hard years.

"Dad." Tyler touched his dad's arm gently.

The moaning halted, and his dad's eyes flew open. The dark brown, usually so honest and kind, was now filled with fear. He reached out a hand and grasped Tyler's. "Son, I'm dying."

2

"I'm not letting him die." Tyler had spoken the words at least a dozen times over the past several hours.

"I'm not letting him die either," Kade responded from the chair beside him in the private ER waiting room at Penrose Hospital.

With sterile walls and furniture, the room smelled of antiseptic. And burnt coffee. When Kade had tried to pour himself a cup, the dripless coffee pot hadn't stopped trickling. The liquid had sizzled and left them with no choice but to inhale the coffee through their nostrils.

Tyler leaned forward, bracing his arms on his knees and his forehead in his hands. A headache pulsed in his temples, and he was doing his best to fight it.

"Hush now," Emberly scolded from where she sat in the blue plastic couch next to their mom, the two of them so much alike with their red hair and brown eyes. "That's enough about dying." She slanted a sideways look at

Mom, then glared back at them as if to tell them they were both idiots for even bringing that up right now.

Emberly was right, as usual.

Dad may have said he was dying, but that was only because he'd been in pain and felt terrible. Once the doctors figured out what was wrong and treated him, he'd be fine. If only there hadn't been a finality to Dad's voice when he'd said he was dying, as if he knew something they didn't.

The door to the waiting room opened, and a young nurse poked her head inside. She glanced around, her gaze landing on Kade, who was wearing a cowboy hat and cowboy boots like he always did. In a flannel shirt that stretched tightly across his shoulders, his brawny body was all muscle. He was slightly taller than the rest of them, his face a little narrower, and his features more boyish, giving him a charm that most women fell for right away. If that wasn't enough, Kade was also a well-known bull rider and had done the rodeo circuit last year. Because of sponsorships, he'd grown even more popular among the womenfolk.

The nurse was eyeing Kade as if she were hoping he'd look back and show interest in her. Normally, Kade didn't mind paying attention to the ladies and doing some sweet-talking. Someone had to do it, and he was usually up for the task. But not today. The situation was too grave to think about anything else, and he didn't give the nurse any encouragement.

The nurse shifted to take in Tyler, assessing him from the top of his hatless head down to his scuffed cowboy boots. He shared the McQuaid good looks, having the same dark hair and dark eyes along with a brawny build. Of course he garnered attention too, but he could admit he had less charm, didn't flirt like Kade, and was much more serious, even severe.

His intense personality hadn't deterred Stephanie. At least, not at first.

He'd met her in college, and they'd fallen in love—or he'd thought they'd fallen in love. While they were dating, she'd always seemed to enjoy their trips from Boulder up to the ranch, even though she was from New York. After they were married, she'd been excited—or so it'd seemed—about using her marketing degree for the ranch.

However, once Wyatt had been born, she'd grown distant. Maybe that had already happened before the birth. Either way, during one of her marketing trips out east, she'd reconnected with a former boyfriend, had an affair, and then returned to the ranch and asked for a divorce.

In hindsight, Tyler could see his role in the failed marriage with Stephanie. In his youth and immaturity, he'd allowed himself to get carried away by her pretty face and beautiful body. They'd had a very physical relationship from the start and hadn't gotten to know each other on a deeper level. If he had, maybe he would've realized how incompatible they were.

If he ever married again—and that was a big *if*—he planned to pick someone from the Park County area—someone used to the mountains and someone who enjoyed the ranch and outdoor activities. Most importantly, this time he wouldn't put so much emphasis on outward appearances and would make sure the physical attraction wasn't the basis for the relationship.

As if sensing his resolve, the nurse's gaze didn't linger on him. Instead, she stepped farther into the private room. "Mrs. McQuaid?"

Clutching Emberly's hand, Mom rose from the couch. "Yes?"

"Your husband is done with the rest of the testing and is back in the ER. He's asking for you again."

Releasing Emberly, Mom nodded and crossed to the door. "How is he?"

"He's comfortable." The nurse opened the door wider and stood back so that Mom could pass by. "The doctor is there and would like to speak to you and your husband."

Tyler stood. "I'd like to be there to hear the doctor."

The nurse's gaze swung back to him, her eyes still filled with interest. "I'm so sorry, but only one person is allowed in the ER at a time."

He nodded. He already knew that, which was why he'd asked for a private room when they'd first arrived. "Is a private room available yet?"

"I think we're still full, but I'll check again." She watched him hopefully, as if she expected him to gush over her for her willingness to accommodate him.

Emberly leveled a stern look at him. "Stop being so pushy, Ty. They're doing everything they can."

He was tempted to stalk past everyone, find the doctor, and demand to know what was going on. But he forced himself to remain where he was, even though everything within him protested more waiting. He wasn't the type of man to sit back and let life pass him by. He was a doer, a problem-solver, the one who made things happen.

Once Mom was gone, he paced the small room like a caged cougar. He killed time by making calls, including talking to Wyatt and telling him goodnight. His son was in good hands with Anson, who was still spunky and energetic enough to handle Wyatt's shenanigans.

Tyler had just finished getting an update from his grounds manager when the waiting room door opened again, and the doctor Tyler had met earlier stepped inside. His expression was grave.

"How is he?" Tyler asked, unable to hold the question back.

The doctor, a young man who didn't appear to be

much older than Tyler, moved to one of the chairs and lowered himself. "Shall we sit?"

"I'll stand." Tyler spread his feet and crossed his arms, trying to brace himself for whatever news the doctor was about to give them.

The doctor steepled the tips of his fingers together, then drew in a deep breath. "Both the blood tests and CT scan indicate that your father has pancreatic cancer."

"Pancreatic cancer?"

"Yes. That's what was causing the stomach and back pain."

Tyler's stomach bottomed out. Silence descended over the room as he and Kade and Emberly stared at the doctor.

Tyler's mind began to spin. He could find a solution to the problem. He always did. "It's all right. Cancer is treatable. There's so much now that can be done to cure it, right?" He didn't know much about treatments, but cancer research had come a long way over recent years.

"You're right." The doctor's expression remained anything but hopeful. "There have been many advancements, and your father's oncologist will have suggestions."

"We'll go to the best cancer hospital," Tyler continued, "hire the best physicians, pay for the leading cures. Anything. We'll do it."

A hand on his arm brought his rambling to a halt.

Emberly had risen, was standing beside him. "What is his prognosis?" she asked quietly.

The doctor rose now too. "The endoscopic ultrasound is scheduled for tomorrow, and we'll find out more after we get pictures of his digestive tract and nearby organs."

"But…" Emberly persisted. "What is your professional opinion?"

The doctor was silent for a beat too long. Long enough for Tyler to know they wouldn't like the answer.

Emberly didn't shift her gaze from the physician. "Doctor, please be honest." At twenty-five, Emberly was turning into a strong woman. She'd been a little down lately because of the recent breakup with her boyfriend. Tyler and all his brothers had realized the guy wasn't right for her. She would see that soon enough too.

The doctor met Emberly's gaze. "It's our hope we've caught the cancer early enough that we can remove it with surgery and chemotherapy. But we won't know what stage he's in until after we get more test results."

"If you had to take a guess," Kade persisted, "what would it be?"

"I'd prefer not to speculate at this point. But I do suggest lining up palliative care at your home so that your father will have the help and comfort he needs when he's discharged."

"Palliative care?" Kade stuffed his hands into his pockets, his shoulders slumping. "Sort of like hospice?"

"We're not giving up and having hospice." Tyler didn't care that his voice was belligerent.

"Of course not," the doctor responded almost too placatingly. "Palliative is the step before hospice to manage the treatment and pain. And since you're a fair distance from the hospital, you'll want to have the appropriate care in place to see your dad through the difficult days ahead."

Emberly was already pulling out her phone. "We'll line it all up. I'll find someone today."

"Only the very best," Tyler insisted.

Emberly slanted him an exasperated look that warned he needed to stop being so high-strung.

When it came to his dad, though, he wasn't about to loosen up. Not even a little.

"Dad's a fighter. Whatever this is, he'll beat it." Tyler wouldn't give up. He'd do whatever it took to overcome the odds. It didn't matter the time or money or effort. He'd find a way to save his dad if it was the last thing he did.

3

Colorado was just as beautiful as she'd imagined.

Kinsey Wingrove peered out the helicopter window to the mountains below, the highest rocky peaks still covered in winter snow, even in May.

"Almost there, Miss Wingrove." The pilot's voice resounded in her headphones.

She gave him a thumbs-up from where she sat in one of the back seats. Then she craned her neck to see the expanse of land spreading out between two ranges that ran from north to south—the one in the east that they were flying over and then the one in the west that rose up just as majestically.

The valley between the two ranges was called Park County and was home to several little Colorado towns including Fairplay, Como, Alma…and Healing Springs, which was the town closest to the ranch where she was headed to start her newest traveling nurse job.

As soon as she'd been called with her assignment, she'd researched the town only five miles from Healing Springs Ranch. Apparently the ranch had been in existence as a homestead from the early days of Colorado in the 1860s, not long after people had flocked to the area for the gold rush. With a hot spring on the land, the owners had opened an associated inn.

Eventually, as the cattle ranch and inn had grown and succeeded, a town had sprung up to cater to the needs of the people living in the area. Now Healing Springs was a posh resort town where people from all over the country came to ski on nearby slopes in the winter and to hike and camp at the reservoir in the summer.

According to everything Kinsey had read, the ranch was even more elite than the town that had been named after it. When she'd first pulled up the website page and seen the prices, she'd choked on her latte and sprayed it over her laptop. Vacationing in one of the beautiful homes at the ranch during peak season cost $16,000 to $20,000 per night. The smaller, but no less elaborate, cabins cost $5,000 per night.

She couldn't imagine who would ever be willing to pay such steep prices for a single night. Obviously people were willing because according to the website, the ranch had no availability for the rest of the year, and accommodations were already filling up for the following year.

The ranch did have an amazing array of activities with stunning views in a secluded mountainous area. From what the website described, guests could participate in horseback riding, rafting, fly-fishing, archery, hiking, and about a dozen other activities that were tailored to the guests' needs by their own personal ranch ambassador. They even had a full-fledged rodeo on site once a week. The meals were apparently also top-rated, the amenities luxurious, and the service outstanding.

Even so, Kinsey hesitated when she had to pay more than $200 a night for a hotel room and couldn't imagine paying $20,000. But from what she'd read, the McQuaids were a very wealthy family themselves and best known because of Brock McQuaid, a famous country music singer. Maybe his stardom had added to the popularity of the ranch.

Whatever the case, she'd gone to some wealthy and elite places during the past four years working for Premier Nurses, since the traveling nursing agency hired only the very best nurses and catered to those who could pay the high rates. Still, she'd never gone to a luxury ranch, and she was not only curious but even a teensy bit excited.

"You'll see Healing Springs Ranch off to your left," the helicopter pilot announced.

She shifted in her seat and peered out the other side. Among the foothills below she could see the stunning log-cabin homes, barns, corrals, ponds, a river, and even a herd of beautiful horses grazing on cleared land.

"It's amazing!" she called back to the pilot.

He tossed her a grin, his gaze lingering on her in the mirror attached above his dashboard. She recognized the frank appreciation in his dark eyes. At five feet seven, she had long legs and was curvy in all the right places. If that wasn't enough to draw attention, she also had waves of highlighted brown hair, bright blue-green eyes, and classic pretty features—high cheekbones, symmetrical round eyes, arched brows, a slender nose, and a narrow chin.

She garnered notice from men everywhere she went. At one point in her life, she'd thrived on such attention. But since Madison's death four years ago, Kinsey hadn't made time for men, had been too busy pursuing her career as a traveling nurse. She'd gotten good at ignoring the interest and looks and compliments. In fact, she'd perfected the ability to act clueless about the attention being lobbed her way. It was easier to fake ignorance than to come up with excuses for why she didn't want to hand out her phone number.

She peered out the window again and feigned renewed interest in the ranch that was drawing closer as the helicopter hovered above a landing pad on a hilltop overlooking the ranch.

As the helicopter landed moments later, she mentally rehearsed all the notes she'd previously studied about her patient, T.W. McQuaid, the patriarch of the family and owner of the ranch. The notes had been sent to Premier yesterday in preparation for Mr. McQuaid's discharge today from the Mayo Clinic in Rochester, where he'd had a distal pancreatectomy, which included having the body and tail of the pancreas surgically removed. According to the records, Mr. McQuaid had also needed to have his spleen taken out, as was sometimes necessary during such a procedure.

Thankfully, the cancer hadn't spread into any of the nearby blood vessels, so Mr. McQuaid hadn't required the more intricate blood-vessel operation. Although the surgeon—one of the best in the country—had removed most of the cancer, there were other tumors elsewhere that would require chemotherapy after recovery.

That was where she came into the picture. Mr. McQuaid was in need of specialized care for the next three to six weeks as he regained his strength and appetite. Currently, the notes indicated he was suffering from delayed gastric emptying and, as a result, had been nauseous and vomiting.

Otherwise, the Mayo pancreatologists agreed that Mr. McQuaid's prognosis was positive. If the man could regain his strength quickly, he'd be able to start chemotherapy earlier rather than later, and that might help him live longer than the usual survival rate of two to five years.

Kinsey braced her shoulders as the pilot swung open

the helicopter door. It was game on. Time for her to prove why she was rated the top nurse in her agency. She'd worked hard to earn her reputation, and she had an incredible success rate with her patients.

This time would be no different. She'd do everything she could to ensure Mr. McQuaid's full recovery.

"Thank you for the ride here." She took the pilot's offer of a hand and hopped down.

"It's no trouble." The young man steadied her, then reached inside for her suitcases, one medium and one small, containing her personal items. She always traveled light. It made living out of a suitcase easier.

The medical equipment, prescriptions, hospital bed, and everything else had hopefully arrived yesterday or earlier today, especially since she'd called the supply company twice to check on the orders. With Mr. McQuaid set to arrive later this afternoon from Mayo Clinic, she intended to have everything ready and be settled in so that she could focus entirely on him.

She hefted her travel bag over one shoulder, glad she'd worn her sweatshirt over her leggings instead of the T-shirt she'd nearly put on before leaving O'Hare. The past few May days at her mom's home in the Chicago suburbs had been warm. She'd almost been tempted to pack her summer clothing for the trip to Colorado.

But now, as a cool mountain breeze brushed at her loose hair, she shivered.

"I still can't believe you're a nurse," the pilot said as he shut the helicopter door. "You're too pretty."

She wanted to roll her eyes. Why did guys think she wanted to hear that she was too pretty to be a nurse? As if pretty women were always stupid.

"Well, I can't believe you're a pilot." She let sarcasm infuse her tone. "You're too young."

She grabbed both of her rolling suitcases and started forward without waiting for him, heading toward the only path on the landing and what appeared to be stairs. She had no idea where she was going, but surely she'd find the main house soon enough.

"Too young?" His voice rose with disbelief. "Now hold on."

She shot him a raised-brow look over her shoulder.

In the middle of opening his mouth to defend himself, he halted and then grinned. "Okay, I see your point."

"What point is that?"

"You're not too pretty?" His answer ended as a question.

She had to bite back a smile.

"Wait," he rushed on. "That's not what I meant. You are pretty. You're just not *too pretty*. Or maybe you are. Maybe you're, uh, just right." His voice held a note of embarrassment—the justice he deserved for his insensitive remark. "I'm a loser, aren't I? I'm sorry for saying I can't believe you're a nurse. You're probably a great nurse. Fantastic. Even awesome."

She wasn't above letting men squirm for a few seconds, but she also wasn't cruel. She paused and tossed him the smile that had come loose, hoping to put him out of his misery. "You're fine. Just forget about it."

He shrugged sheepishly. "I don't know how I'll be able to forget that I just shoved my foot into my mouth. Make that two feet."

She swiveled and started forward but found herself crashing into someone who'd just ascended the stairs and was heading down the path. The momentum from the collision threw her backward.

Since she was still guiding her suitcases, the wheels on both flew off the ground, tipping the suitcases over and flipping her to her back. In the next instant, she found herself lying prostrate, the air knocked from her lungs, staring up at the cloudless blue sky…and a man's face.

"Ma'am, I beg your pardon," he was saying as he hovered above her, his brow creased. "You all right?"

Was she? Even as she struggled to draw a breath into her tight lungs, she did a quick mental scan of her body. She'd landed hard, but she hadn't broken anything, probably would just have a bruised coccyx.

"I'm so sorry," the man said again. "I was in a hurry, was on my phone, wasn't paying attention…."

His dark-brown hair was disheveled and in need of a

haircut, and his tanned face was covered in a thick layer of dark stubble, as if he'd neglected shaving recently. Or maybe he was going for a rugged cowboy look. Either way, he was good-looking, tall, and broad-shouldered, with an intensity that told her he was comfortable being in command.

He held a hand toward her to assist her up. His blue flannel shirt was rolled up at the sleeves, revealing muscular forearms that had a light layer of dark hair. The shirt stretched across hard abs and thick biceps. Faded jeans hugged equally muscular legs, and cowboy boots finished out the ensemble. All he needed was a Stetson and he'd be a true cowboy—the truest she'd ever met.

As she finally drew in a breath, she accepted his hand and found herself being hauled back to her feet in one easy swoop.

He steadied her before taking a step back and raking a gaze over her. "Did I hurt you?"

She winced at the twinge in her lower spine. "I'm just fine."

"Good." His attention didn't linger. Instead, his gaze moved past her as he scanned the helicopter and scowled at the pilot, who was in the process of picking up her luggage. "It's about time."

The pilot shrugged one shoulder. "I'm right on time."

"I asked you to hurry."

"I went as fast as I could."

"It wasn't fast enough."

"I've been in contact with Mom the whole time, and she said Dad is resting comfortably."

Kinsey watched the exchange between the two men. Several things became clear right away. One was that the pilot and the cowboy were brothers, because they shared the same chiseled face with strong square jawlines, broad foreheads, and deep eyes. The second was that they were McQuaids, and their dad was her patient. Third, they were a close family, unlike hers.

"Where's the nurse?" The cowboy glanced at the helicopter again.

A final thing became obvious. The cowboy was just as clueless as his brother when it came to nurses. He probably thought experienced RNs were perky middle-aged women with bobbed haircuts, wearing Reeboks and scrubs.

What was the best way to destroy his stereotypes?

She pressed her hand to her hip so that her sweatshirt hugged her torso and showed off her curves. She balled it up several inches so that he'd also get a good view of her backside and long legs, which always looked sleek and slender in this particular pair of leggings.

She only had to wait a heartbeat for the pilot to cock his head at her.

As the cowboy's gaze swung quickly back to her, she was ready. She gave him her most alluring smile, the one that never failed to melt a man's heart.

He took her in again, this time more carefully. If he was affected by her body or her smile, he didn't give any indication. Instead, he met her eyes directly. "Kinsey Wingrove?"

"Yes, that's me," she said in a too-bubbly voice.

"I'm Tyler McQuaid." The lines in his forehead deepened. "I'm afraid there's been a mistake."

"How so?" She flipped her hair back, shaking her head just enough to draw attention now to her long waves cascading over her shoulders and reaching midway down her chest and back.

His attention flitted to her hair and this time lingered an extra second before falling to her hip and then her legs.

So, he wasn't immune to her womanly curves after all, even though he was obviously trying to be.

He glanced away, then cleared his throat. "We were expecting someone older and with more experience."

"I'm twenty-eight and have been with Premier as a traveling nurse for four years."

"No offense." He met her gaze again. "But I specifically requested Premier's best nurse for my dad's recovery. His life depends on it."

"I am their best. You did read the résumé Premier sent you, didn't you? It highlights my experience, my references, and my success."

"I did. But the paperwork didn't mention your age."

His dark-brown eyes were especially rich and expressive, and at the moment, they were expressing frustration.

She wasn't what the McQuaids had expected. She got that. But usually, even with skeptical patients, she was able to prove herself fairly quickly. "Now that I'm here, you might as well give me a chance."

He hesitated, then shook his head firmly. "Sorry. I can't take any risks—"

"Come on, Ty," the pilot cut in. "What choice do we have now that Dad is home?"

Her muscles tightened. "T.W. is already here?"

The men both nodded.

"He got home earlier than expected," the pilot explained.

"You should have told me." Before either one could say anything more, she grabbed her luggage and started forward at a jog, urgency propelling her into action.

She wasn't on the pathway long before it ended in a stairway. She wasted no time in hefting the suitcases and stepping down.

"Hold on." From behind, Tyler grabbed the handles of both.

"I don't have time to argue with you any longer." She wrenched her luggage free and continued down the steps. "Go ahead and call Premier and request a replacement. In the meantime, I need to get to T.W."

He remained right on her heels. "Fine. Since you're

all we've got, we have no choice."

This guy was something else. She wanted to spin around and give him a piece of her mind. But she was in too much of a hurry to reach T.W. to waste her breath on a rude and egotistical rich man who clearly thought he knew more about medical care than she did.

His fingers closed about the handle of one of her suitcases again. "I can carry your luggage to the house."

She hastened her steps ahead of him, pulling out of his reach. "I'm competent enough to handle my own luggage." She was also competent enough to handle T.W.

She tried to inhale a calming lungful of air. Family members of her sick patients sometimes reacted irrationally. That meant she couldn't take anything they said or did personally. Not when they were stressed and worried and exhausted from dealing with so much.

She had to remember that.

Even so, that didn't mean she had to like Tyler McQuaid. Because she didn't. Not in the least.

4

Heaving echoed from the bathroom in the early morning hour, and Tyler's body tensed with the need to rush to his dad's side.

But the new nurse was with Dad. She hadn't left his side since yesterday afternoon when she'd arrived.

Kinsey. What kind of name was that anyway? He'd never heard it before. Plus, he'd never heard of a twenty-eight-year-old woman having bragging rights to being the best nurse in the best nursing agency in the country.

He was beginning to doubt Emberly's research and decision to go with Premier. How could the company be the best if they sent such young and inexperienced nurses out? How could they be the best if they were forcing him to wait until the end of the week for a replacement?

If they were as good as they claimed, then they wouldn't be making such critical mistakes, and they would have dropped everything to find a much more experienced nurse—someone with more than four years on the job. They certainly didn't have the same philosophy that he did at the ranch about making sure each customer was treated like royalty.

Tyler crossed from the bedroom door to the bathroom, dodging bags and medical equipment and supplies that were strewn everywhere. The disaster was proof that Kinsey wasn't as good as she claimed. So was the fact that Dad still hadn't stopped throwing up.

The stench of it filled the air.

As Tyler paused outside the bathroom door, his sock slipped in something wet. Though the pale light from the bedside lamp didn't reach the spot where he stood, he didn't need any illumination to know what he'd stepped in.

Cringing, he started to back up, then paused. He needed to take off the sock first so that he didn't track vomit through the rest of the room or even the house.

From the main living area off the bedroom, he could hear the faint sounds of Anson making breakfast for both Mom and Wyatt. The voices were quiet and happy, soft laughter mingling with the clinking of dishes.

Tyler could understand Wyatt's steady, happy-go-lucky outlook. The child was still too young to understand the implications of his grandpa's cancer diagnosis and the recent surgery. But Mom? She knew everything—the complications from the surgery, the possibility of infections or internal bleeding, the chance that chemotherapy would have to be put off too long, the risk that the remaining cancer could spread.

Even though the long-term outlook wasn't great, the doctors had said that treatments were improving, and if they remained aggressive in fighting Dad's cancer, he could live a few more years. Tyler was hoping he might be one of the small percentage who overcame it.

Mom claimed she was worried but that she didn't want to borrow trouble from tomorrow. Instead, she said she was taking each day as it came so that she could find joy in every moment she had left with her husband.

Tyler admired her simplistic view, but that wasn't the way he operated.

Sucking in a breath through his mouth, he bent and began to slip his sock off. In the process, he bumped against the bathroom door.

He froze.

Kinsey's voice speaking gently to his dad came to a halt.

He didn't want Kinsey to catch him standing there. She'd think he was eavesdropping or micromanaging her. And he wasn't, was he? He was checking in on Dad, just like he'd been doing long before Kinsey had arrived and taken over.

Quickly he tugged at the soggy sock again. But as his fingers made contact with the slippery wetness, he had the sudden urge to gag.

The bathroom door flew open, revealing Kinsey wearing the same clothing she'd arrived in yesterday, except she was decidedly more rumpled. Her hair was pulled back in a messy bun. Her mascara was smudged beneath her eyes. And her face was pale.

Even so, there was no denying she was an incredibly beautiful woman. That had been evident from the first moment he'd run into her—literally—on the landing pad. Her face was smooth and her features flawless. Not only that, but she had the kind of body that could cause a man to drool—just the right curves, endlessly long legs, and honed muscles.

Not that he was drooling. He'd kept both his mouth and mind closed since he'd met her. No, he was merely acknowledging the facts.

A crease formed in her forehead above her nose. "May I help you?"

As he tried to formulate an excuse for why he was there, his fingers connected with the slimy sock again. He swallowed hard to keep from being sick to his stomach in front of her. But so what if he was sick? He didn't care if he impressed her. He had nothing to prove. Besides, she would be leaving in a few days anyway.

Sucking in a breath, he managed to tug off his sock. He dropped it to the floor, then straightened. "How is Dad doing this morning?"

She cast a glance over her shoulder before lowering her voice. "I've got calls in to two different doctors to try to get a prescription for an antiemetic or neuromodulator to ease his nausea."

"I thought he already had something."

"He has a prokinetic to help with digestion, but it's clearly not working."

Tyler frowned. He didn't like that this woman was trying to make changes. What if she suggested the wrong thing and Dad got worse? "Maybe we should fly him to Penrose and let a doctor there make the decision on what to do for him."

She wiped her arm across her eyes and exhaled wearily.

"I'll have Kade get the chopper ready."

"No." She dropped her arm and glared at him, the color of her eyes more blue than green in the dim lighting of the bedroom. "I can handle T.W. and his care."

"Can you, though?"

"Yes, I'm managing just fine."

"You fooled me." Tyler glanced pointedly at the vomit spot at his feet before nodding to the disaster around the rest of the room.

Her scowl only deepened. "Instead of finding fault with everything I'm doing, maybe you can just mind your own business."

"My father is my business." His voice rose a notch.

She fisted her hands on her hips. "He's my business too."

"Not for much longer."

"I'll continue to do my job until another nurse arrives."

"I don't trust you."

"That's your issue, not mine."

"I should send you away today."

"Even if you did, I wouldn't leave T.W. alone without help."

Somehow their voices had escalated in the quiet of the early morning. He'd crossed his arms and was glaring back at her as fiercely as she was at him.

"Dad?" came a tentative voice from behind him.

Tyler pivoted to find Wyatt standing just inside the bedroom doorway. There wasn't anything about Wyatt that resembled Stephanie. Except for his talkative nature and more open personality.

This summer, she'd invited him to come visit her for two weeks in June. Tyler wasn't thrilled about the trip, but Wyatt seemed to be going through a phase where he was thinking a lot about his mom, or at least thinking about what he was missing out on by not having a mother around.

Early on, Tyler had attempted to persuade Stephanie to work on their marriage. He'd wanted them to get counseling, had admitted he'd been consumed with his work and hadn't spent enough time looking out for her needs, especially when she'd been new to the ranch and everything had been so different from the city life she was used to.

But no amount of pleading had swayed Stephanie. She'd been too miserable to stay. She'd given Tyler full custody of Wyatt—who'd only been an infant and not all that close to her anyway, since she'd traveled so much.

Tyler wished he could say he'd been devastated to lose her. He'd tried to be sad, but the truth was that he hadn't really missed her or their marriage. And that truth made him feel guilty, because he'd broken the McQuaid legacy of love.

Although some people scoffed at the McQuaid legacy of love, Tyler never had. He'd heard the stories passed down through the generations—the stories of the McQuaid men falling fast and hard for their brides and having passionate marriages. His grandfather and his dad had both had that kind of love—the kind where they were all-in, one hundred percent forever. They'd never contemplated divorce and had never given their wives reason to do so. They'd kept their family bonds strong.

Unlike him...

Tyler expelled a tight breath. He'd failed at love, failed at making his wife happy, and failed at keeping their family bonds strong. Ever since the divorce, he'd worked even harder on the ranch to make up for his mistakes, to somehow atone for tarnishing the McQuaid reputation. Even then, he still felt like he'd let down generations of strong men.

At times, he'd wondered if he needed to consider remarriage as a way to repair the legacy, maybe even provide a new mother for Wyatt.

Since he'd already failed once, he was gun-shy about trying again. He didn't want to make the same mistakes, move too quickly, and choose a woman based on physical needs. But even though Wyatt hadn't brought up the whole *woman* thing again, no doubt it was still on the kid's mind.

The boy's gaze now bounced between him and Kinsey. Was Wyatt trying to understand why they were arguing?

Why were they fighting? Tyler hadn't meant to start an argument.

He blew out a rapid breath. "Everything's okay, squirt. Just figuring some things out with Grandpa's nurse."

"With Kinsey?" Wyatt's eyes were round upon the woman. He'd been fascinated with the new nurse ever since he'd arrived home from school yesterday. Of course, he was also concerned for his grandpa's health and was probably worried seeing the normally strong man so weak and sick and helpless.

"Hello, Wyatt." Kinsey smiled at the boy, somehow

easily hiding the strain that had just been tightening her features. "I hope you'll be able to come visit your grandpa when you get home from school later."

"I will." Wyatt's wide eyes took in the big empty bed that was rumpled before he peered at the rest of the messy room.

Mom stepped into the doorway, her gaze downcast as though she was embarrassed to have overheard the argument with Kinsey. "Come on now, Wyatt." She squeezed his shoulder and began to guide him out of the room. "You need to finish your breakfast and be ready by the time Nettie arrives."

Tyler didn't talk to Nettie much, but during their infrequent interactions, she'd hinted that she was interested in him. If he had to pick a mother for Wyatt, she seemed like she would fit the bill. She was kind and caring and loved her own son Levi. Having been born and raised in Park County, she seemed happy with the rural, small-town life. She even had a little shop in Healing Springs that sold locally made jewelry.

With her dark hair and petite frame, she was pretty enough, although he wasn't especially attracted to her since he was partial to tall, willowy women with fairer hair.

But wasn't that his goal? To find someone he wasn't attracted to physically so that he could ensure that his relationship was based on friendship and not on lust?

Wyatt seemed to like Nettie too.

Tyler kneaded the back of his neck. Maybe it was past time to ask her out. Maybe it was past time for him to have a woman in his life, especially because he was having a hard time keeping his eyes off Kinsey.

Even now, as she stood in the bathroom doorway and smiled at Wyatt and Mom, her face was way too pretty. *She* was way too pretty, even after taking care of Dad all night. She probably hadn't gotten much sleep, if any.

Guilt pricked him. Whether Kinsey was the right nurse or not, he needed to offer her breaks from her caregiving so that she could sleep and eat.

Of course, during the introductions yesterday, Mom had let Kinsey know she would help with the caregiving. She'd also told Kinsey she could use the kitchen and help herself to whatever food was there.

Kinsey had thanked her, but from the looks of things, she'd been too busy to think about her own needs. In fact, her bags were still by the bedroom door where she'd dropped them yesterday. She hadn't even taken a few seconds to deliver them to her room next door—Dad's office that they'd cleared out so a live-in nurse could be close to him in the event of an emergency.

At a sound from the bathroom, Kinsey disappeared inside. Mom and Wyatt returned to the kitchen, and Tyler followed them. He finished helping Wyatt get ready for school, then ushered him out the door into Nettie's waiting SUV.

When he returned to the kitchen, Anson was almost finished cleaning up breakfast, but at Tyler's request, the old cowboy put together a plate of eggs, bacon, toast, and coffee. As Tyler carried it into the bedroom, Dad was lying in bed with his eyes closed and Kinsey was in the process of taking his pulse.

Guilt nagged Tyler again. He'd been too hard on Kinsey—shouldn't have questioned her abilities so bluntly and shouldn't have admitted that he didn't trust her. He'd handled the situation poorly.

She finished with the pulse, jotted the numbers on an iPad, then finally glanced his way.

He held out the plate and mug. "Here. Have something to eat."

She hesitated, her expression wary.

"You've been working hard and doing your best," he whispered. "I'm sorry I was rude about it."

She studied his face, as if testing the sincerity of his words. Then she took the plate and mug. "Thank you. For the food and apology."

He nodded.

She blew at the coffee, then took a sip.

"Why don't you eat, unpack, and catch a few hours of sleep." Tyler lowered himself into the bedside chair. "I'll keep an eye on Dad for a little while."

About to take a bite out of the toast, she paused. "Is this because you don't trust me to do a good job?"

"It's because you probably haven't slept in twenty-four hours."

"I'm used to going without sleep."

"You'll be a better nurse and more alert if you aren't exhausted." Even though he wanted to convey compassion, his words were too firm, like he was lecturing one of his employees.

Her eyes started to narrow.

"Wait." He held out a hand to stop her from responding. "That came out wrong." Every time he opened his mouth around this woman, he said something stupid. What was the matter with him?

She resumed her eating and watched him, clearly waiting for him to expound.

"You look like you could use a break, that's all."

She glanced down at herself, then tossed the toast back onto the plate. "You're right. I should change."

"That's not what I meant either." Inwardly he groaned. "You look fine...I mean, you look more than fine. Even finer than fine." Shoot. What was he saying? He needed to stop talking.

She quirked a brow. She probably thought he was not only an ogre but also an idiot.

"Listen." He couldn't keep his voice from tensing or from radiating the frustration at himself. "Go rest for a while. That's all I'm saying."

She seemed about to protest, then pressed a hand to

44

her forehead, weariness radiating from her body. "All right."

He expelled a tight breath.

She shuffled toward her suitcases.

He jumped up and crossed the room. She'd refused to let him carry them yesterday. The least he could do now was put them in her room. In fact, he should have thought of that earlier.

As he grabbed hold of the handles of both, she held on for a second longer before releasing them, her shoulders slumping. Silently, he carried them next door and deposited them on the end of the new bed.

Their interior decorator had been the one to transform the home office into a suitable space for a nurse. The aspen bedposts and other lightwood furniture had been accented with shades of blue. It was classy and matched the design throughout the rest of the house.

Kinsey had followed him into the room and lowered herself to the edge of the bed.

"Take all the time you need," he offered.

"Thank you."

He waited a second, not sure what more he expected. More conversation? Or maybe he wanted to make sure she was okay.

He really was letting this woman fluster him, and he needed to put an end to it. Without another word, he walked to the door and exited.

5

Kinsey couldn't remember the last time she'd felt so miserable.

At the buzz of her phone, she rolled to her side and tried to sit up, but her head throbbed like the bass on a car stereo turned up too loud and on repeat. She had no appetite and was weak and dizzy.

The illness had started shortly after she'd started caring for T.W. At first she'd wondered if she'd picked up a virus on the plane from O'Hare to Denver, but it hadn't taken her long to realize she was experiencing altitude sickness—an adjustment to the lower air pressure and lack of oxygen that came at the nine-thousand-plus-feet elevation of the high country of Colorado.

"Ugh." She couldn't afford to be under the weather. Not on her first full day on the job. And not with how sick T.W. was. He needed someone to monitor him carefully, especially in order to get the nausea under control. She'd gotten him to drink the electrolytes in the oral rehydration solution, but it wasn't staying down any more than the other fluids had. She would have to start an IV.

Thankfully, the equipment she'd asked for was all here. She hadn't had the time to sort through it, but she'd seen the IV pole, the pump, and the tubing.

The trouble was, she could hardly stand, much less insert an IV line.

Her phone buzzed again with an incoming call. She pried open an eye, pushed herself halfway up, and pawed at the bedside table until her fingers connected to her phone. The screen read 11:35, which meant she'd been lying down for at least three hours. She should feel better by now. But if anything, she felt worse.

Her friend's name was flashing across her phone. "Hi, Pippa," she answered in a croaky voice.

"Girl, you sick?" came Pippa's loud question over the speaker.

"No." Kinsey tried to sound normal. "Just a little altitude adjustment is all."

"Don't you be trying to fool me now." Pippa's voice was even louder. "You sound sick."

Kinsey flopped back onto the bed, unwanted tears stinging her eyes. She glanced at the closed door, then dropped her voice to a near-whisper. "I'm not doing so well, Pippa."

47

"That's what I figured."

"You did?"

"Yes, ma'am," Pippa was saying, still too loudly. "T.W.'s son Tyler called yesterday and chewed me out for sending him such a young pup." As a co-owner of the company, Pippa still traveled as an RN, but mostly, she oversaw the scheduling and needs of the rest of the traveling nurses.

"I'm not surprised he complained. He hasn't been too happy with me so far." Even though Tyler McQuaid had told her to rest and to take all the time she needed, she had to get up and start working again. After she'd boasted to him that she was the best nurse working for Premier, what choice did she have?

So far, all she'd done was show how incompetent she was. It hadn't helped that T.W. had arrived before her and she hadn't been able to set up his room the way she wanted or put away the supplies and equipment. It also hadn't helped that the Rochester doctors hadn't given him an anti-nausea medication. The past long hours of taking care of him had been a disaster.

"Don't worry about what that guy thinks," Pippa bellowed. "He obviously doesn't know one end of a syringe from the other."

Kinsey's mind filled with the image of Tyler from earlier in the day when he'd handed her the plate of breakfast and a mug of coffee. His brown eyes had been especially brooding and intense. But that hadn't stopped her from noticing how good he'd looked with a dark layer of scruff covering his jaw and chin and his hair combed back and still damp from a shower.

Even if she didn't like him, that didn't mean she couldn't admit he was handsome—if a woman was into the country-cowboy type, which she wasn't. She'd always gravitated toward athletic men who were easy-going and funny, probably because she was driven and serious and such men tended to balance her out.

"Whatever the case, I need you to find me a replacement." Kinsey closed her eyes against the sunshine streaming in through one of the room's large windows.

"Already told that young man I don't have anyone else available until the end of the week." Pippa's tone turned sassy. "And he told me he would find a different agency who was more accommodating."

"He did not." Kinsey pushed up, the same irritation at him from earlier in the day prodding her.

"Um-hmm. He did."

"Then he really does hate me if he's unwilling to wait."

"I told him you're in high demand and that I had to cancel one of your regular jobs so you could take the assignment with his father."

"And...?"

"Like I said, he wouldn't know the sharp end of a

needle unless it poked him."

Kinsey smiled. This was why she needed Pippa. Because the dear woman not only knew how to make her smile in the most disheartening of situations, but she always had her back. It had been that way since Madison had required palliative care during her last year of life and Pippa had been Madison's nurse.

Kinsey had been working at Edward Hospital in Naperville at the time, since she'd wanted to stay close to home and close to her younger sister, especially once the leukemia had spread and Madison had dropped out of college.

At the time, their mother and father had done everything they could to find additional treatments, new tests, even experimental medication. Kinsey had done all she could too. In the end, Madison had died and left them all brokenhearted and even more fractured than they'd already been.

Through it all, Pippa had been there for Kinsey, as solid and steady as a mountain. She'd been the one to encourage Kinsey to apply to become a traveling nurse so that she could move on and find new purpose instead of staying stuck in the past the way her parents were.

Pippa had been right. Kinsey had found purpose in helping a variety of patients through their medical issues. Even though the long months and years of watching Madison suffer and eventually die had been extremely difficult, Kinsey was beginning to see the truth—that her hardships and pain hadn't been a waste because now she could empathize with her patients and their families so much more easily.

"If you're sick, girl, I'll come replace you myself." Pippa's voice now radiated concern. "I'll send you back to the Binghams. They love you."

The older wealthy couple who lived in Portland, Maine, did love her and treated her like family. Even so, Kinsey wasn't ready to give up yet. Maybe it was because she already liked T.W. Maybe she wanted a chance to prove herself, to show Tyler and everyone else she wasn't a failure. Or maybe she needed to stand up for young nurses who deserved respect.

Kinsey forced her body up to a sitting position and blinked back the dizziness. She could do this. She had to do it. "From everything I've read about altitude sickness, it should go away within a few days." At least, she hoped it would.

"You don't have to do this."

"I know. But I'd like to stay for as long as I'm able."

Pippa was quiet for a moment. "Fine. I trust that you won't do anything to jeopardize yourself or the patient."

"Thank you."

"You know I'll do anything for you," Pippa said passionately.

"And I'd do the same."

Kinsey chatted with Pippa only a minute longer before ending the call. Then, even though she felt like she'd been given a dozen vaccines all at once, she forced herself to get out of bed. After taking ibuprofen and guzzling water, she washed up and changed into fresh clothing.

Her head still pounded, and she felt lightheaded, but she felt better than she had last night. Maybe her body was beginning to adjust to the higher altitude, or maybe the sleep had helped. Either way, she needed to check on T.W.

Hopefully the new prescription had been delivered by the local pharmacy. If it had arrived, then she would start the IV and administer it to him right away.

She tiptoed out of her room and down the short hallway that led to the main bedroom. The house was quiet—almost too quiet. While she hadn't glimpsed much of the house in her haste to get to T.W. yesterday, she'd seen enough to know that it was gorgeous both inside and out—a mansion made of logs and furnished with tasteful western decor.

As curious as she was to take a better look, her patient took precedence. She'd come to assist T.W. on his road to pancreatic cancer recovery, and she wouldn't let anything distract her from that.

She tapped lightly on the bedroom door to announce her arrival before pushing it open and stepping inside.

T.W.'s wife, Leah, was sitting in the chair by the hospital bed, reading. At the sight of Kinsey, she smiled as she closed her book and placed it on the bedside table next to a vase of flowers.

Kinsey had partly expected to find Tyler on duty, but she wasn't about to complain that he was gone and Leah had taken his place.

"How is T.W.?" Kinsey crossed the room, assessing her patient in a sweeping glance. His eyes were closed and mouth slightly open, and he seemed to be sleeping with even respirations. The bright light pouring in from the large windows illuminated the dark circles under his eyes and his sallow complexion.

Upon meeting T.W., she'd immediately seen his resemblance to his sons in the broad build and handsome features. He'd aged well. At fifty-eight, his dark hair was threaded with only a smattering of silver, and his face was etched with only a few lines near his eyes.

"He's asleep," Leah whispered as she took in her husband's face, "and getting a break from the dry-heaving."

"Good," Kinsey whispered back as she stepped beside T.W. and gently touched his radial pulse. She counted the beats and was relieved when the palpitations were normal.

Leah stood. "Is he okay?"

"Yes, perfect."

Some of the tension seemed to ease from Leah's face. Free of makeup and with her wavy red hair tied back loosely, she had a natural beauty that defied her age too.

From the moment of meeting T.W.'s wife, Kinsey had been able to tell just how much the woman cared for her husband, especially from the way she looked at him and how she tenderly hovered over him.

Kinsey couldn't remember ever seeing that kind of love in her parents, not even in her youth, before Madison's diagnosis. If there had ever been love between her parents, it had evaporated completely once Madison had gotten sick. Her parents had done nothing but bicker over Madison and the treatment plans. They'd both only wanted to find a way to save their daughter, but through all the stress, demands, and uncertainty, they'd ended up destroying their already fragile marriage.

"How are you doing?" Leah asked, her eyes filled with kindness.

"The sleep helped." Kinsey picked up the new prescription sitting on the dresser, relieved it had finally arrived.

"I have some medication for altitude sickness that you could take."

"My sickness is that obvious, huh?" Kinsey made her way to the bed.

"You're not the first. We always have a handful of guests who have trouble adjusting to the altitude the first few days. I keep the medicine on hand." Leah tugged a small bottle from her pocket and held it out. "It'll bring you some relief."

Kinsey reached across the bed and took it. She'd do anything at this point to help herself so that she didn't turn out to be an utter failure. Even if she only had a week left, she was determined to do her best and show this family—namely Tyler—that she was a competent nurse.

Where was the cranky cowboy, anyway? Besides Leah, Tyler had been at T.W.'s side the most. Two of the other siblings had been in and out of the room. Kinsey had learned that the helicopter pilot, Kade, was the youngest and that Emberly was the McQuaids' only daughter. Both had been friendly and welcoming...unlike Tyler.

"Since T.W. is sleeping, why don't you go get something to eat?" Leah cocked her head toward the open door. "I can stay with him a few more minutes."

Kinsey hesitated. Even though she wasn't particularly hungry, she needed to take the altitude medication with food. She may as well get it over with, especially since she didn't intend to wake T.W.—not if he was resting peacefully.

"Anson stepped out to run some errands," Leah continued, "so please help yourself to anything."

Kinsey followed the hallway until she found herself at an enormous dropdown living room. Filled with beige leather furniture, including a large sectional, the area was wide open to a loft above. The far wall was mostly windows, with a sliding glass door that led to a balcony.

Rustic wooden barrels served as end tables. A wagon wheel covered with a glass top made a unique coffee table. Decorations of wood carvings, a lasso, horseshoes, and antlers were tastefully placed around the room.

Even though she wanted to walk around and examine each item, she found herself drawn to the large windows and sliding glass door. As she halted in front of them and took in the view, she inhaled a breath at the vastness of the valley that spread out for miles and the mountains that rose on the opposite side.

It was stunning, the kind of panorama that defied words—one a person would never tire of seeing. While she'd visited some pretty places as a traveling nurse, she could admit this was one of the finest.

She turned around and took in the great room again and the kitchen beyond. With an open concept, the kitchen had a center island and a separate eating nook that overlooked the view as well. Everything was a blend of stainless steel and beige and browns highlighted with more western decor.

If all the other houses on the ranch were as beautiful as this one, maybe she could understand why the rental rates were so high.

After a few more moments of taking everything in,

she made her way to the kitchen and peeked in cupboards and the refrigerator. She'd had to learn to be bold when it came to living with other people, especially because she preferred to stay with the patient rather than finding a hotel or other accommodations.

As she opened a high cupboard and spotted saltines, she lifted on her toes to reach them. While the thought of eating wasn't appealing, the bland crackers would help settle her stomach.

Her fingertips brushed against the box, but even straining, she couldn't grasp it. Without a stool close by, she climbed onto her knees on the counter like she used to do as a kid when she needed something from a high cabinet.

She balanced herself, then reached for the box again.

"What are you doing?" A clipped voice came from behind her.

Startled, she wobbled. At the same time, she glanced over her shoulder to find Tyler standing several feet away, his thick arms crossed, a scowl leveled at her from beneath the brim of a Stetson.

She shifted back, but her swift movement made her lightheaded and dizzy, and she could feel herself starting to lose her precarious perch. She attempted to grab on to the open shelf in front of her, but it slipped through her fingers, and she started to fall backward.

6

Tyler lunged for Kinsey. He hadn't meant to scare her, but apparently he was a bigger idiot than he'd realized.

As she wobbled, he tried to steady her, but she was already toppling backward. He did the only thing he could think of. He caught her in his arms, so that he somehow ended up holding her like he was a groom with his bride, stepping over the threshold on their wedding day.

He gave a quick shake of his head at the unwanted image. Or maybe it wasn't so unwanted after all. Maybe subconsciously, his mind was telling him he needed to give more than a passing thought to the idea of remarriage.

Not to Kinsey. No, of course not. Absolutely not. Perhaps he should get serious about asking Nettie out. She'd flirted with him again this morning when she'd picked up Wyatt for school. Tyler never flirted back, but maybe he should give it a try.

"Oh bother." Kinsey grabbed on to him. "I'm such a klutz."

"No. It was my fault. I startled you."

"Yes, you did." Her tone held indignation as she glared at him. Were her blue-green eyes filled with contempt?

After their not-so-great start, she obviously didn't like him.

"I'm sorry." If he took a poll of the words he'd used most frequently with her so far, *I'm sorry* would win. "I should have warned you I was standing in the kitchen before lobbing a question at you."

"It was more of an accusation." She was clutching at his shirt and hanging on to him as though she was afraid he might decide to drop her to the floor like a bug he wanted to squash.

"I definitely asked a question." He remembered walking in from the rear entrance, hearing the rummaging through the cupboards, and being surprised to see her on the counter, perfectly at home, almost as if she'd grown up here and had every right to take whatever she wanted.

"Fine. Technically, 'What are you doing?' *is* a question, but the tone of your voice was accusing."

She was right. He had accused her because he'd overreacted to her being on the counter.

"I'm sorry." The words fell out again. "I don't know why I even asked in the first place. You have every right to be in the kitchen."

He didn't care if she hunted through the cabinets. She was probably getting something for his dad. If she was getting a snack for herself, that was okay too.

Had he asked because he'd been mad at himself for the bolt of attraction he'd felt when he'd noticed her incredible body as she'd stretched up to reach something in the cabinet, showing off her tight jeans?

He shouldn't have looked. Then when he did, he should have forced himself not to let his gaze linger over that nice backside. A backside that his arm was now pressed against. A backside that was just as firm as it had looked.

Shoot. He was being a class-A jerk by focusing on a woman's physical appeal and making that the center of his thoughts instead of keeping all of that locked away where it belonged.

He started to loosen his grip. He had to put her down. There was no reason to keep on holding her like she was a coveted prize he'd just won at the county fair. But as her gaze skittered across his face and took him in, he couldn't make himself move.

She wasn't making an effort to free herself. Not that she was thinking the same thoughts about him that he was of her. Far from it. She was probably trying to figure

---

out how a thirty-two-year-old man could be such a jerk.

Had he lost his mind around her? Because she was so pretty?

He let his gaze skim her face too. As with every other time, he was fascinated by her flawless beauty. Up close, her lashes seemed longer and thicker, her skin was toned and looked as soft as velvet, and her lips were perfectly rounded.

What was he doing?

With a half growl, he lowered her to her feet.

Her grip in his shirt remained tight for an extra beat. Or maybe he was only imagining that. Either way, he took a step away from her, and at the same time, she released him and backed up.

She stared at his chest.

Was the air between them strangely charged? Maybe he was imagining that too.

She waved at the box of crackers still in the high cabinet. "Should I try climbing up again? Or would you like to be my knight in shining armor and get the crackers for me?"

"Knight in shining armor?" He released a scoff, then he swiped the box down and handed it to her.

"Thanks." The word was cold and curt. She tucked the box under her arm and began to open and close more cupboards, ignoring him as if he weren't in the room anymore.

61

He wasn't used to women ignoring him, and he had the sudden urge to get a reaction from her. "When I said take your time earlier, I probably should have specified that didn't mean take all day."

"Whew. It's a good thing you clarified," she scoffed. "Because I was planning to run off in a minute and join one of the nature painting sessions first."

She had obviously researched the various activities on their ranch. Was she mocking their painting program? They had an expert instructor, and guests loved the experience of riding out into nature, setting up an easel, and capturing the view with their own artistic flare.

Kinsey slammed one cupboard closed and wrenched open another. Apparently finding what she was looking for, she took down a glass, then pressed it against the water dispenser in the refrigerator door. Then she tipped a pill out of a medicine bottle, popped it in her mouth, and drank the water. When finished, she placed the glass on the counter and slapped down the bottle of pills.

If her flashing eyes hadn't been enough to alert him to her anger, the banging was.

Without another glance his way, she swiped up the box of crackers and stalked out of the kitchen in the direction of Dad's bedroom.

Tyler didn't want to watch her walk away, but his gaze slid her direction anyway.

Her hair, now hanging loose, swished with every firm

step. And her hips swayed just a little, although she probably didn't realize it. Too bad his body had to notice it. But it did, and his gut sparked like steel striking flint.

He gave himself a mental shake. It had been a long time since he'd had such a strong reaction to a woman. Maybe not since Stephanie, and look where that reaction had gotten him.

Besides, Kinsey was a spitfire. Maybe that was causing the unusual sparks.

As she turned from sight, he picked up the bottle of medication she'd left behind. The acetazolamide that his mom kept on hand for guests having trouble adjusting to the thin air of the high country.

Was Kinsey suffering from the altitude? Was that why she'd looked so sick this morning?

With a fresh wave of guilt hitting him, he set the bottle down, then tapped the lid. He'd done it again. He'd been thoughtless and insensitive and clueless. He should have guessed from her symptoms that she was sick from the altitude.

They encouraged most guests not to do any of their vigorous activities until their bodies had a chance to acclimate. Most took it easy the first day or two.

But of course, Kinsey had landed with both feet, rushing here and there at full speed. She'd worked hard since arriving. He could admit that. But she'd clearly tried to do too much too soon, and he should have cautioned her.

He stared in the direction of his dad's bedroom. Did he need to go and apologize to her again?

Why, yes. Yes, he did.

With a sigh, he started down the hallway. As he entered the room, Kinsey was already at Dad's bedside and holding a basin as he vomited. He had nothing left to spit up, but he was still nauseous.

Worry tightened Tyler's chest as it had since they'd brought Dad home. He'd wanted Dad to stay in a rehab facility for a while longer to be closer to the professionals who could help him. But Dad had insisted on returning to the ranch, had claimed he'd disrupted everyone's lives long enough.

The physicians had all assured Tyler that Dad was well enough to leave, that he was recovering, and that he was a strong and determined enough man who would likely heal quickly.

Dad leaned back against the mound of pillows and closed his eyes. Mom gently stroked his hair, and he lifted a hand toward her—the sign that he wanted to hold her hand. She settled her other hand in his.

Their love for each other was always so beautiful to see. But it was also a constant reminder of how he'd failed to love Stephanie in the same way.

Kinsey put the basin on the end of the bed, then reached for the IV pole. "Your new medicine should kick in soon, Mr. McQuaid, and you'll be feeling better in no time."

"Remember to call me T.W., darlin'," Dad said weakly. "You're making me feel old with all that *Mr. McQuaid* stuff."

Kinsey laughed lightly as she unwound the tubing and situated it on the IV pole. "We don't want that, especially because the honest truth is that you don't look old enough to have five grown kids."

Dad opened his eyes and gave Kinsey a smile. "You're real sweet, you know that?"

"I can be sometimes. But don't let that sweetness fool you. I can be pretty tough sometimes too."

Dad turned his gaze upon Mom's face. "Reckon a little bit of sweetness and spiciness go together real well. Never is good to have all one or the other."

Mom leaned down and kissed him tenderly on the cheek. He lifted their intertwined hands to his mouth and kissed her hand just as gently.

Kinsey had paused and was watching the couple.

Tyler braced a shoulder against the doorframe. He was used to the displays of affection. But what did she think?

As if hearing his unasked question, her gaze darted his way before returning to the IV pump, where she began to press buttons.

Dad followed Kinsey's look to Tyler and raised his brow as though to question Tyler. But about what?

Tyler shrugged in what he hoped was nonchalance.

Dad narrowed his eyes in a silent rebuke. "I'm real blessed to have found the love of my life."

"You are blessed." Kinsey's voice held sincerity.

Dad squeezed Mom's hand. She squeezed back before kissing him on her way out of the room.

After she was gone, Kinsey made quick work of inserting the IV in Dad's arm.

"Do you know something else?" Dad asked when she finished.

"What's that?" Kinsey tore off a piece of tape and placed it over the spot where the tube entered Dad's vein.

"I keep hoping and praying my kids will find the love of their lives." Dad's voice held a tinge of regret. "But none of them have yet."

"I'm sure they will eventually." This time Kinsey's answer felt more like a platitude, as if she didn't quite believe the words, probably because she didn't believe *he* would find someone.

"Reckon with my getting cancer," Dad continued, "all my kids would be open to moving things along more quickly so that I can see them all happily married before I die."

"Da-ad." Tyler pushed away from the doorframe. "Come on. You're not dying anytime soon." At least, he hoped not.

"We don't know how long I have." Dad pinned him

with a hard look. "And I want to see you happy before I die."

"I am happy."

"You don't know what true happiness is—not until you find that special someone you can't live without." Dad's face lit with a life and energy that hadn't been there in weeks—not since before the cancer diagnosis.

Even though Tyler wanted to object again, he bit back his protest. If his dad found hope in thinking about his children getting married, then Tyler wasn't about to say anything to crush that hope. He couldn't. In fact, he'd do just about anything to keep that hope and his dad alive, even if that meant facilitating a relationship with a woman.

Tyler took a deep breath. "You're right, Dad. I haven't found someone I can't live without. If my finding a wife will keep you fighting for life, then I guess I need to start looking."

"You have to do more than just look."

"Fine. I'll get married if you promise to get better."

"I can't promise I'll get better any more than you can promise you'll fall in love. Neither is guaranteed."

"But we can both agree to do our best."

His dad was halfway sitting up, the conversation obviously important to him, as if Tyler getting married was the ultimate cure for his cancer.

Tyler knew that wasn't really possible. But maybe there was something powerful about hope. What if hope was a stronger drug than anything a doctor could prescribe?

"All right," Dad said.

"All right?" Tyler began crossing to the bed.

"All right, I'll give it my best. As long as you promise to do the same with finding the love of your life."

Tyler nodded. "You have a deal."

Dad stuck out his hand. "Let's shake on it."

Tyler stopped at the end of the bed and hesitated. "Should we hash out a few terms first?"

"Like what?"

"Like you have to accept my ideas for your health care."

"Then you have to accept my ideas for finding your love."

"Fair enough."

"I'll take to heart your advice, and you'll take to heart mine."

"Okay." The bargain seemed harmless enough. After all, Dad didn't know that many young women. In fact, from what Tyler knew about the history of the area, the men always had outnumbered the women.

Tyler reached out and clasped his dad's hand in a firm shake.

Dad squeezed hard, then grinned. "Excellent. Already I feel better."

Kinsey flicked a finger at the syringe as she squeezed

out the last of the medicine into the IV. "It's a good thing Tyler's such a charmer." She couldn't keep the sarcasm from her voice. "He'll be married in the blink of an eye."

Dad's gaze swung to Kinsey, his eyes rounding in surprise, then filling with mirth. "Sounds like you already know Tyler well."

"It didn't take long to figure him out." She softened her words with a half grin.

"He has a lot of growl but no bite."

"Are you comparing me to a dog?" Tyler stuffed both hands into his pockets, suddenly self-conscious but not sure why.

"More like a bear." Dad was watching Kinsey now as she retrieved a thermometer and wiped it down. "On the outside, you act like a grizzly, but on the inside, you're a big teddy."

Tyler scoffed.

Before he could answer, Dad spoke again to Kinsey. "So, darlin', do you have a fellow yet?"

Tyler bit back a sigh at Dad's not-so-subtle attempt at matchmaking. "Really, Dad?"

"What?" Dad turned innocent eyes upon him. Innocent but tired. The conversation wearing him out.

"Time for you to get some rest." Tyler backed up several steps, half hoping Kinsey would answer Dad's question about whether she already had a *fellow*.

But she was busy typing notes on a tablet.

"And time for me to get some work done," Tyler added, although reluctantly. He'd worked virtually the past few weeks while he'd been with Dad at the Mayo Clinic, and he'd kept up with the most pressing issues.

However, a whole heap of work had piled up for him—decisions on expansion projects and renovations, a meeting with the accountant, the purchase of the new mares, and most recently, a case where the state was questioning their family's right to own the hot springs.

Normally he thrived on the problems, tackling each one as it arose as if it were a wild mustang that needed taming. Lately, the problems were galloping all over him, so that he'd had more headaches in the past few weeks than he'd had in the past year.

"Believe it or not," Kinsey said without pausing or looking up from her notetaking, "your dad won't go to pieces without you here."

Dad chuckled, even as he closed his eyes. "I like you, Kinsey."

Tyler wished he could say the same. "You rest up, and I'll be back later." He started across the room.

"You'll work on your end of the bargain?" Dad's question, so filled with hope, made Tyler stumble.

"Of course," he called over his shoulder. Should he text Nettie today and schedule a date? Or maybe he needed to have Kade or Emberly set him up with a friend.

They'd both offered at one point or another over the past couple of years. If that didn't net good results, he could always try an online dating app—although that would be his last resort.

He'd promised his dad he'd do his best to find the love of his life. He wasn't exactly keen on the agreement, but handshake or not, he'd do whatever it took to help Dad heal.

7

Kinsey liked Wyatt a whole lot better than Tyler.

"And over there you can see the archery range." Standing beside her on the deck, Wyatt pointed beyond the corrals to what appeared to be targets but were difficult to see through the trees, especially in the fading light of evening. "My dad says I'm real good."

"I'm sure you are."

"You can come watch me sometime if you want."

She hesitated. She didn't want to encourage Wyatt into thinking she could do things with him. T.W. was her priority, and she needed to make sure the boy knew that. On the other hand, she was leaving next week when her replacement arrived. So what harm was there in letting the child think they could be friends? She'd be gone soon enough.

"I'm also good at shooting a pistol."

"A pistol?"

"Yup. I can hit the hundred-foot target already."

Did the ranch let children his age handle real guns? Maybe they only had BB guns or some other kind of fake gun for the younger ones. At least, she hoped so. She'd seen more than a fair share of accidents over the years than to approve of children handling firearms.

The seven-year-old was a miniature version of his dad in his looks, but that was where the similarities ended. Wyatt was easygoing, talkative, and sweet, unlike Tyler, who was definitely a grizzly bear and not a teddy bear.

She'd only talked to Wyatt a few times since arriving, and she liked the little boy more each time he sought her out.

After spending all afternoon and evening with T.W. without a break, Leah had insisted that Kinsey take some time to sit down and eat. Anson had still been in the kitchen when she'd come out, and had been overseeing Wyatt's homework sheet.

The older cowboy had fixed her a meal in no time. Then Kinsey had brought her plate to the deck to watch the sunset while she ate. Even though the air was chilly and the shadows long, she'd breathed in deeply, trying to quell the dizziness that still bothered her, although the medicine was helping tremendously after having it in her system over the past hours.

Only a few bites into a grilled-chicken sandwich, Wyatt had slipped out onto the deck, and he'd been chattering away ever since.

"For a while I thought I might wanna be a cowboy when I grow up and be just like my dad." Wyatt was attired in miniature cowboy boots, a fringed vest, and a cowboy hat with his dark hair curling up underneath. "But then I decided I wanna be a bull rider like my uncle Kade."

Kade, the pilot? "He's a bull rider?"

"Yup, he's got lots of belt buckles to show for it."

"He seems nice." She'd only seen Kade a couple of times since she'd started taking care of T.W. While he loved his dad, he didn't have the same intensity as Tyler and wasn't so bossy.

"My uncle Brock likes to play the guitar and sing. But I can't whistle a tune to save my soul."

She laughed lightly. His uncle Brock was much more than a guitar player and singer, but the boy obviously hadn't grasped the extent of his uncle's fame yet.

"I never could whistle either." She finished her last bite and set her plate aside on the glass patio table. "But then I learned a trick that helped me."

Wyatt plopped down into the wicker chair next to hers, his brown eyes so rich—like Tyler's.

Tyler did have really great eyes. They were like a double espresso—dark and intense and strong with the power to melt a woman's insides.

Not *her* insides. Okay, well, maybe a little melting

happened on occasion around him. It was hard not to get sucked into those eyes when she looked closely at him. Most of the time, however, she was too annoyed with him and his arrogance to feel any melting.

"Can you show me your whistle trick?" Wyatt peered up at her with such anticipation that she couldn't resist him.

"You have to press your tongue against your bottom teeth like this." She opened her mouth and showed him. "Then you have to curl your tongue into the shape of the letter u."

Wyatt pressed his tongue, then curled it. He blew out air for long seconds before a sound slipped out. It was a whistle so soft that even a baby mouse could squeak louder.

But Wyatt jumped up from his chair, his face alight with excitement. "I did it!" He pressed and curled his tongue again, and this time the whistle was slightly louder.

"That's right." She smiled at the genuine delight that shone from his eyes.

For a moment, she felt sorry for him—sorry that he didn't have a mother to give him all the love and care and guidance that he deserved. From everything Kinsey had picked up during the conversations so far, she'd learned that Tyler's ex-wife lived in New York City and was remarried to the third or fourth man since leaving Tyler.

Her only child was Wyatt, but Wyatt wasn't close to her, since she'd left when he was an infant.

"Listen." He hopped up and down, then proceeded to whistle even louder.

"You caught on quickly."

His grin widened as he started to pucker again, but then his gaze shifted, and he glanced behind her toward the sliding glass door. "Dad!" He darted toward Tyler, who was stepping outside onto the deck.

Tyler had taken off his Stetson, and now a hat ring encircled his hair. Even with his flat hair, he was too ruggedly good-looking with the scruff on his jaw, his dark blue T-shirt pulled tightly across his chest, and his chin jutting with determination.

He was just too hot for any woman's heart rate to handle, including hers.

She was sure if she stopped and took her palpitations, her pulse would be off the charts.

"Guess what! Guess what!" Wyatt reached Tyler and nearly tackled him with enthusiasm.

"Whoa now." Tyler lifted the boy up into the air as effortlessly as if he were a paper airplane that he was about to launch from the deck to the open hillside.

"Kinsey taught me to whistle!"

The beginning of Tyler's smile faltered, and he cast a glance in her direction, a slight crease in his brow the sign that he wasn't pleased. Why? Because he still didn't trust her? Because she was being overly familiar? Because he thought she might develop a relationship with his son only to have to end it?

Whatever the case, Tyler didn't say anything to her and instead focused on the little boy. He had Wyatt show him his new whistle several times and listened with an endearing raptness. Then he sent Wyatt inside, telling him he'd be right in so that Wyatt could practice some more while getting his bath.

As soon as the glass door closed behind the boy, Tyler crossed his arms and peered down at her, that crease deepening and his eyes narrowing. Why did his shoulders have to strain against his shirt? Almost as if they were pushing to be free of a shirt altogether.

Before he could chastise her, she leaned back in her chair. "You're welcome."

"I didn't say thank you."

"I saved you the trouble."

"I don't consider saying thank you *trouble* when it's warranted, which it wasn't."

"I taught your son how to whistle. I deserve a bonus for that."

"I didn't ask you to teach him." He ground out the words, his scowl deepening.

"Well, too late." She pushed up, ready to be done talking with Tyler even though they'd only just started. "Even if I could take back teaching him, I wouldn't."

The setting sun was casting a brilliant red-orange hue over the western range. It cast a glow over Tyler, too, making him appear even taller and fiercer.

"You're a temporary nurse to my dad." With a glance toward the sliding glass door, Tyler dropped his voice. "You're not here to spend time with my son."

"I don't generally make a practice of ignoring children who are being friendly with me."

"And I don't appreciate when women befriend my child in order to attract my attention."

She scoffed. "If you think I want your attention, then you clearly have no clue how to read women."

"After overhearing the conversation I had with my dad about marriage, maybe you're trying to weasel your way into my family."

She stiffened with the sudden urge to smack him across the cheek. "I wouldn't marry you if you were the last man on earth." Her voice came out low and angry.

Tyler didn't budge, continued to glare with his thick arms crossed.

She folded her arms and mimicked his stance, even though she knew doing so was immature.

For a long moment, neither of them moved.

At a tapping on the sliding glass door, they both glanced at it to find Wyatt pressed up against the glass, his lips in a pucker with a whistle.

She relaxed her tight expression and gave him a

thumbs-up.

Tyler nodded at the boy. "I'll be right there, Wyatt. Go on and wait for me in your room."

The little boy nodded back and then waved at her before racing off.

When he was gone, she turned back to Tyler. "If you don't want your traveling nurse to interact with any of your family members, then you may have to consider providing them an alternate housing option so that they have a place to go when they're not on duty."

He stared at the sliding glass door for a few more seconds, then heaved a sigh. "You're right. I can't expect you to ignore Wyatt."

She liked that Tyler was so quick to admit when he was wrong. He might be arrogant at times, but he also had a humility that seemed to balance him out.

"Listen, Tyler." She let her anger dissipate now too. "You should know that I am well aware of how impressionable young children are, and I don't want to lead them on."

A breeze rattled the pinecones in a nearby spruce before the draft raced across her, sending goosebumps up her arms.

His gaze shifted to her arms, and he immediately began to shrug out of the flannel shirt he was wearing over the T-shirt. Before she could protest, he was draping it around her shoulders.

She didn't necessarily want to wear his shirt, but if he was being polite, she needed to be too.

Was this the tender, teddy-bear side of Tyler that T.W. had mentioned?

"Thank you." She wrapped the flannel closer, breathing in a woodsy pine-and-cedar scent. Earlier in the day, when he'd caught her after her tumble from the counter, she hadn't paid particular attention to his cologne.

But now, as his shirt enveloped her, she was surrounded by the manly scent, and the warmth of his body remained in the fabric too.

He rubbed at the back of his neck, as though the stress and well-being of his entire family rested on his shoulders. Maybe it did. Maybe as the oldest child, he felt responsible for his dad and the rest of his family.

She'd felt that too when her family had been going through her sister's leukemia battle. She'd wanted to swoop in and rescue everyone. She'd tried to control the situation and make everything better for as long as she could. Eventually, she'd learned that letting go sometimes took more courage than hanging on.

Her lessons hadn't come easy and had taken plenty of time. Now, when she was working with patients and their families, she couldn't forget people had to fight for life first before deciding when death was inevitable and that they had to let go. It was her job to walk the journey with them wherever they were and to be there to encourage and help, and she couldn't rush their steps.

Normally she was patient and kind and able to handle even the angriest of family members. So why was she having trouble keeping her emotions under control with Tyler?

"You only have to put up with me for a week." She picked up her plate with the remains of her meal. "Then hopefully you'll get a nurse that you approve of more than you do me."

With that, she crossed to the door, slid it open, and escaped from Tyler's overpowering presence.

8

Even with the harness, carabiner, and belay rope holding him securely, Wyatt wobbled like a newborn calf on the two-by-four wooden beam of the new high suspension bridge.

"You got this, squirt." Tyler stood only a foot behind Wyatt.

"Only a little farther!" came the encouragement from the ropes course manager, Cooper Hayes, below on the opposite side of the suspension bridge. Cooper peered up at them from behind dark reflective sunglasses, his baseball cap on backward and doing nothing to shelter him from the slant of evening sunshine.

"Good job, Wyatt!" shouted Anson, who was sitting in a camping chair next to Cooper, whittling away on another mushroom.

Tyler hadn't done their usual Friday night activity since that fateful night earlier in the month when they'd been fly-fishing and he'd gotten the call from Mom that Dad had fallen in the bathroom.

Since today had been the last day of school before summer break, Wyatt had wanted to do something to celebrate, and Tyler had suggested trying out the new bridge that had been completed as part of the ranch's high ropes course. Wyatt had been thrilled at the option.

"I'm not afraid, Dad." Wyatt cast him a glance over his shoulder, a wide grin lighting up his face.

"It's all right if you are." Tyler was harnessed in too and wearing all the same gear. "Sometimes a healthy fear is a good thing and keeps us from being reckless."

"I promise I'm not reckless." Wyatt stepped onto the next slat, the bridge swaying again.

"That's good."

From their perch above the trees, they had a great view of the ranch and his family's house sitting proudly on the high hill.

It was a far cry from the old Victorian-style house that his grandfather had lived in, one built in the 1870s across from the original Healing Springs Inn. Tyler had only seen pictures of the old house and inn, since they'd been torn down when his grandfather had been in charge of the ranch. When so many other ranches in Park County had gone broke, his grandfather had renovated and rebuilt, turning their high-country land into a destination resort that appealed to a wealthy clientele.

Grandfather's decision—along with the discovery of oil on their land—had saved their ranch and also allowed the family to buy up acreage for miles around. Dad had enlarged the business and modernized the resort, increasing their popularity so that lodging was always full with long waiting lists.

When Tyler had taken over as general manager, his ideas had propelled the ranch's reputation to the next level, making it even more elite and modern, so that now they were drawing in celebrities and prominent guests from around the country, bringing in multimillions every year and making Tyler one of the wealthiest men in the country for his age.

"Look!" Wyatt called. "There's Kinsey!" Wyatt lifted a hand off the rope railing and pointed toward the house.

Sure enough, Kinsey had stepped through the sliding door and onto the deck. She was too far away for them to see her clearly, but it was obvious she was taking a rare break from Dad.

She was a tireless and dedicated worker. That was easy to see after the past few days of watching her on the job.

Had he been too swift to pass judgment on her when she'd arrived? A part of him knew that he had. Even if she'd gotten off to a rough start that first day, it hadn't been her fault. She'd been thrown into Dad's care without any time to prepare, and she'd been sick and had kept going.

Yes, she was still too young and inexperienced. But she had done all right.

Okay. Maybe she'd done more than *all right*. She'd actually done a fantastic job alleviating Dad's nausea and pain so that he was slowly regaining an appetite. She was getting him out of bed a little each day to walk around. Even when he was in bed, she had him doing light exercises, lifting weights, and other PT and OT therapies. She never took no for an answer from Dad, always encouraging him to do more than he thought he could but never pushing him too hard.

She was also friendly and personable with both Dad and Mom. She cared about them as people and clearly didn't see her duties as a checklist of things that needed to be done.

A part of Tyler was beginning to suspect she hadn't been boasting when she'd claimed she was Premier's best nurse. Had he made a mistake in requesting someone else older? What if the replacement wasn't as proficient and dedicated?

"I like Kinsey, Dad," Wyatt called, loud enough for both Cooper and Anson to hear—because both of their faces tilted quickly upward and fixed on Tyler, waiting for his reaction.

He shot them both a glare.

Anson responded with one of his gap-toothed grins, which crinkled his leathery skin. Cooper's dark sunglasses hid his eyes, but nothing masked the guy's curiosity.

Did every staff member on the ranch know about the new nurse and how attractive she was?

Wyatt waved in the direction of Kinsey, but she'd taken a seat on the deck, and they couldn't see her as well.

"I told you not to bother her." That night when she'd taught Wyatt how to whistle, Tyler had later cautioned the boy to be careful not to interrupt Kinsey's work, hoping to deter him from spending too much time with her.

Wyatt took hold of the rope rail again. "She told me I'm not bothering her. I think she likes me."

"I'm sure she does like you. But you have to let her do her job. That's why she's here."

Wyatt brought his foot forward so that both were now on the same slab. Tyler started to move to the next board directly behind Wyatt.

"If you're nicer to her, she might start liking you too, Dad."

Tyler halted, his precarious perch swaying a little too much. How exactly should he respond to that?

"She'd make a real nice mom."

"Whoa now, squirt." Shoot. The conversation had gone from bad to worse fast. He had to figure out a way to get Wyatt to stop thinking about Kinsey. "We barely know her."

"It's all right." Wyatt placed his foot on the next step.

"I asked her if she had a boyfriend, and she said no."

Tyler wouldn't admit to his son that he'd been curious about Kinsey's relationship status and was strangely satisfied to know she was single. Instead, he had to chastise the boy for prying. "Listen, Wyatt. You can't go asking—"

"She's real pretty, don't you think so?"

"Yep!" Anson called from below, his grin widening. "Your dad thinks she's a pretty little filly."

Tyler tossed the old cowboy another glare. "We don't refer to women as horses. That's derogatory."

"Fine. She's a pretty little thing. That better?"

"We don't call women a *thing* either. That's objectifying them."

Anson's grin faltered—probably because he didn't know what *objectifying* meant.

"Listen," Tyler continued, "all you have to say is that she's pretty. That's all it takes."

Anson's lips curled up again. "See, I knew you thought she was a pretty little thing."

Tyler bit back a sigh.

Wyatt halted only a few feet away from the end of the bridge. "Even though she said she's not looking for a new boyfriend, I figured you could change her mind."

This time Anson's crotchety chuckle echoed in the air, and Cooper smirked up at him.

All Tyler could do was shake his head at the two of them.

"What do you think, Dad?" Wyatt hopped the last couple of boards and grabbed on to the landing like the seven-year-old daredevil that he was.

Tyler made quick work of finishing the ropes course and joining him on the landing.

"Wanna give it a try?" Wyatt smiled up at him with hopeful eyes. "You got that bargain with Grandpa to keep."

"Yep. That bargain!" Anson called as he started whittling on his carving of the mushroom.

Tyler tugged on Wyatt's harness, making sure it was still secure and buying himself some time to think of an answer. Finally, he sighed. "Kinsey's leaving in a few days." He hadn't told anyone else yet about the replacement, but Wyatt obviously needed to know the news.

Wyatt shrugged. "Tell her she can stay."

So much for squelching the kid's enthusiasm for Kinsey.

"The truth is, squirt," Tyler started, "Kinsey and I, well, we'd never get along even if she did stay. So I'll have to find another way to keep that bargain with Grandpa."

Wyatt studied Tyler's face for a long moment, his brown eyes growing serious. Then he nodded. "Okay." As if the matter were settled, he lowered himself to the first rung of the ladder and started to descend.

Tyler could only watch him, stuffing away the disappointment that the boy hadn't protested a little bit harder.

9

She had only two days left at Healing Springs Ranch.

Kinsey opened the miniblinds and let the early-morning sunshine into the room.

T.W. squinted through his reading glasses at the laptop in front of him.

It was a good sign that he was feeling well enough to want to work again. After the past weeks of not being able to do much, dipping his toes back into his business was good for his mental well-being and gave him some purpose and reason to recover...probably a more realistic reason than having his kids get married.

She could admit she was going to miss being with T.W. when she left. She'd grown fond of the McQuaid family in the short time she'd been there. The place had a wonderful homey feel to it, one that she missed because she hadn't had a home of her own since she'd started working with Premier.

"Hey, Dad." Tyler poked his head into the room.

Kinsey ignored him as she did most times he was around. Mostly he ignored her too. Thankfully, he'd stopped watching her every move and questioning the care she was giving to his dad. And thankfully, he spent the majority of his time with his dad when she was busy doing other things.

But there were the inevitable times when he was around. Like now...on Memorial Day, when he was probably taking the day off work. Hopefully he would be gone all day spending time with Wyatt.

T.W. peered over the rim of his glasses at Tyler. "Just looking at some of the first-quarter reports—"

"I've got a surprise for you." Tyler stepped into the room and smiled.

Tyler was pompous and overbearing at times, but he did have a nice smile, which didn't show itself all that often—primarily when he was with Wyatt. She had to give Tyler credit for being a good father, which was no surprise since he'd had such a good role model with his dad.

T.W. took off his reading glasses and gave Tyler his full attention, probably because he realized how rare the smile was too.

Tyler moved aside and then nodded at someone in the hallway.

Another man filled the doorway—a man just as

broad-shouldered and muscular as Tyler, although slightly shorter and more rugged-looking.

Kinsey's heart flipped. It couldn't be…

But it was. *The* Brock McQuaid was standing there looking as handsome as all his pictures portrayed him. Even more handsome, actually. He had the McQuaid chiseled features, strong square jawline, and wavy dark-brown hair beneath a cowboy hat. But his face was scruffier than Tyler's, his eyes wider, and his expression softer. His dark T-shirt was tight, with a tattoo peeking out from one of the short sleeves.

Of course there was his trademark crooked grin. It was a heart-stopper.

"Hey there, Dad." Brock's smile wavered as he surveyed his dad in the hospital bed, probably seeing how pale and thin and weak he looked.

T.W.'s grin made an appearance. "Well, look what the cat dragged in."

"Yep." Brock crossed to the foot of the bed. "Had the day off and wanted to drop in for a visit."

Drop in. Because that's what famous country music stars could do. Fly on their private jets to Colorado for the day.

Kinsey knew she was staring, but she couldn't stop herself.

As if sensing her stare, Brock shifted and took her in. "Hey, darlin'."

"Hi." The word came out almost as a squeak. The second it did, she wished she could take it back and say it normally, especially because she could feel Tyler watching her now too.

Brock's smile widened. "Didn't know we had another guest, and such a pretty one at that."

"This is Kinsey Wingrove." Tyler's brows fell into an ominous V. "Dad's nurse."

"She's a real gem." T.W. beamed at her.

Kinsey was grateful that at least T.W. liked her and was willing to say nice things about her. Because Tyler sure didn't and sure wouldn't.

"Pleased to meet you, Kinsey." Brock was studying Tyler's face now, his eyes alight with interest.

"She's got me feeling better already," T.W. said.

"That's because you're a good patient." She hoped her voice sounded normal this time. She wasn't used to meeting famous people on the job. It was definitely a first and a story she'd relish telling Pippa. Her friend would be jealous, since she loved country music.

Brock's brow quirked at his brother in a silent question. "We appreciate you taking such good care of our dad, don't we, Ty?"

"We do." Ty raised a brow back.

T.W. was watching his sons interact, amusement lighting up his eyes. "I sure do wish I could interest one of you in dating Kinsey."

"Oh no you don't." Kinsey shook her head sternly at T.W. and started toward him. "Don't you start playing matchmaker with me, young man." After his so-called bargain with Tyler the other day, she'd expected him to start setting Tyler up with women. She just hadn't expected him to try it with her.

T.W. winked at her. "Course, that's my second job."

"Not with me, it's not." Kinsey pressed her lips together.

"You still dating that singer, Brock?" T.W. turned his grin onto his son.

Brock had circled around to the chair by T.W.'s bedside and was lowering himself. "Yep. I'm still dating *that singer.*"

Kinsey didn't have to ask who they were talking about. Brock's image was splashed all over the internet with the pop-singing sensation Ainsley Rose. They looked beautiful together.

Brock leaned back and tipped up his hat, revealing more of his handsome face. "Since I'm off the market, guess that means Ty's gonna have to date Kinsey."

Tyler shook his head at the same time Kinsey released a scoff.

"Don't forget your bargain with me, son." T.W. cut in before Tyler could offer a protest.

"I'm not."

"Bargain?" Brock was watching Tyler again. "What

kind of bargain?"

"That he's gonna get married."

Brock's grin inched up higher. "I see."

"I said I'd consider it." Tyler spoke hastily. "Because Dad said he'd like to see his children married before he— before he—"

"Dies." T.W. finished the sentence.

A gravity fell over the room.

Kinsey reached for the blood-pressure cuff on the edge of T.W.'s bed. "Now, stop the talk of dying. You're doing just fine. It'll be a long while before you die, which is a good thing because it'll take Tyler a long while to find someone willing to put up with him."

The room grew suddenly silent. Too silent.

In the process of unraveling the cuff, she froze. Oh bother. She'd spoken too boldly. It was one thing to lob half-truthful jokes with Pippa and other friends. But she shouldn't be doing so with her patients and their families. She was out of line.

"I'm sorry…"

Before she could formulate the rest of her apology, laughter burst out behind her.

She spun to find T.W. and Brock both laughing and looking directly at Tyler, who was standing unmoving by the door.

At some point, Leah had arrived in the room and stood in the doorway. Wyatt wasn't anywhere in sight, probably busy with Anson. Kinsey was relieved the boy hadn't been there to hear her critical remark about his dad. She would have been mortified.

As it was, she was embarrassed enough.

"She's good," Brock said through a chortle. "Real good."

"Yep." T.W.'s voice rang out with happy breathlessness.

Tyler had to be spitting mad at all the teasing.

Kinsey chanced a peek up at him. At the twitch of his lips upward into the beginning of a smile, she eased out a breath.

He wasn't offended. Thankfully. In fact, he seemed to be taking the teasing good-naturedly.

Maybe it was for the best that she was leaving the ranch in two days after all. She might have avoided offending Tyler this time, but with the way they seemed to rub each other the wrong way, the friction was bound to cause problems eventually.

10

Tyler forced himself to smile at Nettie as she brought her clunking SUV to a halt at the back of the house.

He'd been making himself smile each morning he saw her, ever since he'd made the bargain with his dad about trying to find a woman to marry. But the smiling wasn't getting any easier.

Beside him, Wyatt was whistling. The only time he stopped was when he was sleeping.

The early-morning sunshine streamed through the branches of the towering spruce trees that covered the hill behind the house. The warmer, summer-like weather had melted the last piles of snow that had lingered in the cold shadows of the hillside.

"Good morning!" Nettie smiled back as she rolled down her window.

Levi had already opened the back door, and Wyatt was bounding forward, eager to start his first day of horsemanship camp. Wyatt had talked about the camp all weekend. Even yesterday on Memorial Day, when Brock had surprised them with a visit to spend the day with Dad, Wyatt had still talked of little else.

Now decked out in cowboy gear—hats, boots, and even spurs on the heels of their boots—the boys started chattering about the two weeks ahead of them filled with everything from trick riding to roping to horse care.

"Thank you for taking Wyatt." Tyler stepped up to the SUV and to Nettie.

She pushed her sunglasses up into her dark hair that was as smooth and sleek as a horse's mane. Her nose was sprinkled with a layer of freckles, and her bright eyes were framed with dark lashes. "It's no trouble, Ty. I'm happy to do it."

"Mom said she'll pick the boys up this afternoon when camp is done."

"Are you sure?" Nettie scrunched up her nose. "I might be able to sneak away from the shop."

"No, it's fine. She said she could." His mom had been a huge help over the years in caring for Wyatt. Actually, both his dad and mom had poured out their love and support for him and Wyatt. Even though Wyatt was getting older and didn't need quite as much caretaking, the boy's schedule was always full and busy.

"Could she drop Levi off at the store?" Nettie asked.

Before Tyler could answer, Wyatt poked his body out

of the back window and waved both hands wildly at someone coming up the driveway. "Hey, Kinsey!"

Yes, indeed, Kinsey was out running. From the perspiration and flush on her face, she was obviously finishing up.

She halted at the sight of the SUV, took in Tyler's position at the window beside Nettie, then shifted to look at Wyatt. "Hey there, kiddo." She offered the boy a wide smile, one she never used around Tyler.

"I'm leaving for horsemanship camp!" Wyatt called.

Wyatt had told Kinsey he was going at least a dozen times over the past few days, and already once this morning when she'd finished Dad's breakfast routine and had come out into the kitchen to deposit dishes in the sink. Wyatt had been in the middle of eating his breakfast and had been excited to see and talk to her as usual.

"Have fun!" she replied as she lifted her ball cap slightly and wiped her forehead with the back of her hand.

Tyler only glanced her way for a second. But that one glance was enough to turn up the temperature of his blood. She was just too blasted hot. Every day. But especially when she was in her running clothes. The loose Nike shorts showed off her long legs. Today she had on a tank top that revealed her toned arms and shoulders, and she wore her hair in a high ponytail that came out through the back of the hat.

She was just as stunning when she was out running as she was when she was taking care of Dad. Was there ever a time when she didn't look beautiful? If so, he hadn't seen it.

Of course, he was doing his best *not* to look at her. He didn't want to be that kind of man. He'd seen the way the ranch hands had sized her up the first time she'd gone running.

She'd only just started over the weekend, probably because she'd acclimated to the altitude. She hadn't run far or long, but she had taken the road past the barn, and he'd happened to be there checking on the newest foals when she'd gone by.

He'd been surprised at the anger that had flared inside him when the few young men in the corral with him had paused their work, leaned against the split rails, and stared at her. He'd barked at them to get back to work and warned them not to make any comments about his dad's nurse.

But they had a short while later when they thought he wasn't listening. They'd remarked how pretty she was and then dared each other to ask her out. He'd almost stepped back into the barn and told them he'd fire them if they talked to her. Fortunately, he'd stopped himself from the irrational urge.

After all, he'd basically fired her the day she'd arrived, and now, after working there one week, she was leaving tomorrow. He'd finally told Kade, who'd agreed to fly her to the Denver airport while picking up the new nurse.

Nettie, who had been studying Kinsey, shifted her attention back to Tyler. "How is your dad this morning?"

"He's making good progress." Thanks in no small part to Kinsey's tireless efforts. She was always up late at night tending to Dad, and she was always up before anyone else to take care of him. She worked hard all day too, and she hadn't taken a single day off since arriving a week ago.

Of course, Mom gave her breaks, like right now while she went for a run. And Tyler sat with his dad in the evening for a couple of hours to give her another break. Other than that, she worked around the clock, probably only getting five or six hours of sleep a night.

His gaze shot to her again, even though he didn't want it to. She'd reached the back door and stopped again to stretch. With her back facing them, he had the perfect view of her endless legs and the shorts that were almost too short.

"Wyatt talks all the time about Kinsey." Nettie was watching his expression now.

Was she trying to decide how he felt about Kinsey? Whether or not he was attracted to her?

It was hard not to be. Not when she was beautiful both inside and out.

He'd tried to limit his interactions with her, especially

because it seemed that he could never say the right thing around her. He'd made sure to stay as polite as possible and to keep the conversations about his dad.

She'd done the same. At times, she'd even seemed to go out of her way to avoid being around him, and that was fine with him. Although, he couldn't deny that he liked her sharp wit. She wasn't dull. That was for sure.

She lifted one of her lower legs in a stretch so that her running shoe bumped her backside.

As if sensing his gaze, which was now riveted to her, she glanced over her shoulder. And caught him staring.

Shoot.

He shifted a step closer to the SUV, braced a hand on the roof, and leaned in toward Nettie. "If you're free next Saturday night, I'd like to take you out to dinner."

She'd already lowered her sunglasses, so he couldn't see the reaction in her eyes, but as her lips curled up into a bright smile, he could sense her pleasure. "I'd love to."

"Good." From the corner of his eyes, he could see Kinsey openly watching their interaction.

For a brief second, he was embarrassed he'd asked Nettie on a date so impetuously and in reaction to Kinsey. But maybe that had been the push he'd needed to take the next step with Nettie.

He didn't linger much longer. After having taken yesterday off to spend with Brock and the rest of the family, he had meetings lined up most of the day and needed to get down to the ranch offices that were congregated on the first floor of the lodge. But before leaving, he stopped into Dad's room with a fresh cup of coffee for both of them.

His dad was alert and talkative as Tyler sat beside him. "I love that little tyke's whistling," Dad insisted. "And I'm sure gonna miss him when he heads off to New York City."

"I doubt Stephanie would protest if I told her Wyatt can't come." Tyler wasn't sure why Stephanie had insisted on having Wyatt visit this year when she never had before. The most time she'd spent with Wyatt was five or six days over Christmas as well as his spring break in Aspen. Anson had gone with Wyatt and supervised his care, and the old cowboy was planning to accompany Wyatt to New York City too.

With the hospital bed raised, Dad took a sip of his coffee, his brow creased and his eyes filled with concern. "I think Wyatt's starting to figure out that he doesn't have a mother."

"He has a mother."

"Not one who lives with him like most of his friends."

Tyler paused with his steaming mug against his lips. Maybe Wyatt had been oblivious when he'd been younger. But now that he was beginning to understand how most families were designed, he probably realized something was missing in his life.

Kinsey breezed through the door to Dad's room, showered and changed and full of life. At just the sight of her, his dad's whole demeanor changed. His eyes lit up, the worry lines eased from his forehead, and a gentle smile turned up his lips. "How was your run?"

She didn't acknowledge Tyler as she returned Dad's smile. "It's getting easier every day."

"How many miles did you go today?"

"I managed five." She crossed to the bed, attired in her usual jeans and T-shirt.

"You'll be back up to ten in no time."

Kinsey shot Tyler a sideways glance, arching an eyebrow in question.

What question, though?

He gulped his coffee and shrugged one shoulder.

She faced him squarely and braced both hands on her hips. "I take it your son has neglected to tell you that I'll be leaving tomorrow?"

"What?" With his mug halfway to his mouth, Dad halted and stared at Kinsey.

"Tyler doesn't think I'm an experienced enough nurse." As Kinsey spoke the words, she stared directly at Tyler. "So he called my company and asked for someone else to come and take care of you."

His dad shifted to stare at him too. "I don't understand. Kinsey's excellent."

"I realize that, but I want you to have the best nursing care possible—"

"Kinsey is the best. I don't want anyone else but her."

"It's too late. I've already made the arrangements."

"Cancel them." Dad's voice was firm.

Tyler knew that determined tone, had heard it lots of times over the years. When Dad wanted something, he could rarely be swayed from it. That forceful focus had helped him build the ranch into what it was, but on a personal level, that forceful focus was difficult to handle.

If Dad wanted Kinsey to stay, he wouldn't relent. But would his health continue to improve if Kinsey stayed? Or would they eventually wish they'd found someone better?

Dad's hand began to shake, and the coffee sloshed over the edge.

Kinsey braced her hand against his. "It's okay, T.W. You'll do just fine and like any of the nurses that Premier sends. I guarantee it."

Dad pushed the coffee into her hands, then sagged against his pillows and the bed. "You're the only nurse I want taking care of me."

"I like being here with you too." She spoke quietly, gently. "But you're doing fine, and you're going to be better in no time."

He closed his eyes, his features turning haggard, almost as if in the blink of an eye he'd aged ten years.

A battle waged sudden war within Tyler. Kinsey was good at what she did. She'd more than proven herself.

But he'd been counting on her leaving. He was already struggling to keep from thinking about her. After Brock's comment yesterday morning about dating Kinsey and then more teasing throughout the day, she'd never been far from his mind. He couldn't imagine having her here for another week, much less a month or more.

"Admit it, Ty." His dad opened his eyes and pinned him with a stern look. "You're attracted to Kinsey. That's why you don't want her here."

"No." Tyler pushed to his feet, causing the chair to scrape against the floor obnoxiously. How had his dad guessed his thoughts so easily? Was his attraction to Kinsey that easy to see? "I'm going out on a date with Nettie."

Dad's eyes remained shrewd, as if he could see every emotion raging through Tyler. "Then if you're not attracted to Kinsey, it shouldn't bother you if she stays."

"It's not attraction, T.W." Kinsey broke into the conversation. Thankfully. Because it was embarrassing to talk about his attraction to her while she was right there by the bed, listening to every word. "We actually don't like each other very much."

Dad's gaze bounced between them as if he was trying to figure out what the true nature of their relationship was.

"She's right," Tyler insisted. "We can hardly be in the same room and remain civil."

"That's because you're afraid to get involved with someone like her."

Was he afraid?

Tyler shook his head. "Think what you want, but that's not true." Very few things frightened him. Certainly not a traveling nurse, no matter how gorgeous and spirited she was.

"If you're not afraid, then prove it. Let Kinsey stay and be my nurse."

Tyler could feel the coils wrapping tighter around him. His dad was trapping him. That's what he was doing.

Tyler rolled his shoulders, as if that could somehow free him from the trap.

Kinsey's staying wouldn't have to change anything. He could limit his time around her and keep his interactions to a minimum, just like he'd already been doing.

Besides, he had the date lined up with Nettie for Saturday night. He'd focus on getting to know Nettie, and that would start to occupy his mind and push out thoughts of Kinsey.

He started across the room. "If it's that important to you to have Kinsey as your nurse, then I'll call and cancel the replacement."

"Do you want to stay, Kinsey?" his dad asked.

"I'd love to stay and help you through the rest of your

recovery." Her voice was sincere. "But I don't want to cause tension between you and Tyler."

"It won't cause tension, right, Ty?"

Tyler paused in the doorway and swallowed the tension that was already clamoring for release. "I'm sure Kinsey and I can behave like mature adults."

Kinsey didn't reply.

"Then it's settled," Dad said quickly. "She's staying."

"Fine." Tyler waved a hand but didn't want to turn, too afraid of looking at Kinsey, too afraid that the attraction Dad had accused him of would be written all over his face.

Like it or not, Kinsey was in his life to stay. At least for a few more weeks.

11

Kinsey gripped the reins of her horse and tried to relax as she did another loop around the corral.

"You're doing great!" Wyatt called from his perch on the top rung of the fence next to the young ranch hand who'd been patiently instructing her.

Kinsey bent and patted her mare's head, not caring that she'd been given the oldest and slowest horse for her first day of riding lessons.

"Just remember to relax your back and arms." Wyatt spoke maturely, as if he were twenty-seven instead of seven.

Ducking her head, Kinsey bit back a smile. Her lesson had been almost over when Wyatt had bounded up to the corral after arriving home from his horsemanship camp.

Since he'd been excited to see her on top of the horse, she'd stayed on for a little longer, although she needed to start getting ready for a fancy dinner in the lodge.

Apparently everyone dressed up in their best for the weekend meals, which were followed by dancing. Emberly had insisted that Kinsey go with her.

T.W. had actually been the one to demand that Kinsey take a break. After working since her first day here without any personal time, he'd encouraged her to take one day a week for herself.

Kinsey knew she needed the day of rest, but for some reason, admitting it seemed like a weakness. She'd finally only agreed because T.W.'s second youngest son, Dustin, had arrived home unannounced yesterday and said he would spend Friday with T.W.

Even then, she'd still hesitated until T.W. had lined up Emberly to take her around the ranch and pamper her for the day. They'd toured the ranch on bicycles and then ended at a spa, where Kinsey had enjoyed a hydration wrap, massage, and facial. After that, Emberly had taken her to Brook Barn, where they'd eaten lunch in the rustic dining room there.

In the afternoon, Emberly had arranged for her to go on one of the medium-hard guided hikes that was only a couple hours long. Kinsey had tagged along with a group of the guests and loved getting out into the wilderness and hiking to even higher elevations, where the views were stunning. After a week and a half in Colorado, she'd acclimated and hadn't had too much trouble with the trek, either up or down the trail.

Upon her return, she'd learned Emberly had lined up horseback-riding lessons for her. Now, as Kinsey finished, she was even more grateful to T.W. and Emberly for providing a relaxing and fun day for her to enjoy the ranch. She'd needed the break more than she'd realized.

As she directed the mare toward Wyatt, he grinned at her proudly. "I knew you could do it."

She allowed herself to smile back, but at the outline of a man in the shadows just inside the barn, she held herself in check. She didn't have to see the man's face to know who he was. The powerful build and commanding presence belonged to only one man on the ranch—Tyler McQuaid.

Even though he'd agreed to T.W.'s wishes to keep her as the primary palliative care nurse, Tyler hadn't been thrilled by the decision and had agreed only reluctantly.

At least he'd made an effort to be cordial to her over the past few days, hadn't been so cold and silent. Or maybe T.W. was the one trying to include her, and Tyler wasn't shutting her down so quickly.

She didn't want to lose the truce that had settled between them, and she had the feeling she would if she wasn't careful about how much time she was spending with Wyatt. Tyler had made it clear on one of her first days at the ranch that he didn't want her crossing the boundaries with his son, and she needed to respect that.

"Time for me to try to dismount." She tugged on the

reins, and the horse ambled to a halt.

The ranch hand hopped down from the fence and started to jog toward her. "Hold on. I'll show you how it's done."

"No you won't." Tyler stepped out of the barn and scowled at the young man.

The ranch hand halted midway through the corral and glanced from her to Tyler and back, his brows rising with confusion.

"I can help her, Dad," Wyatt called as he started to climb down.

"Stay put, squirt." Tyler stalked out of the barn, his expression stormy. "I'll take care of it."

Kinsey hesitated in her saddle. She wanted to tell Tyler she'd rather have the ranch hand or even Wyatt teach her how to dismount. Honestly, instead of interacting with Tyler, she'd prefer to try it on her own and risk falling flat on her face. But she also didn't want to make a scene, especially in front of Wyatt. He didn't need to know how much she disliked his dad.

But Tyler spanned the distance quickly. As he reached her, he took hold of the bridle and then ran his hands across the creature's muzzle. From the surety of Tyler's hold and his ease with the horse, no doubt he'd grown up spending his days in the corral and going to horsemanship camps too.

He rubbed the horse for a moment before glancing up

at her. "Ready?" His eyes were a lighter brown than usual. Or maybe they just seemed that way in the late-afternoon sunshine.

"If you are."

He nodded at her stirrup. "Most horses are trained to have their riders dismount on the left, so you'll want to lift your right foot out of the stirrup first."

She took her foot out.

"Swing it over the horse."

She shifted in the saddle but started to slip.

His hand closed around her leg and braced her. "It helps to grab on to the mane."

The horse's loose hair rustled in the wind. "Won't it hurt her?"

"Not at all. She's used to it."

Kinsey wrapped her fingers through the mane and then raised her leg again. This time the hold helped to balance her.

"Lean forward." Tyler's instructions were gentle, almost kind. He was obviously a good teacher and used to being in the role.

She did as he said.

"Now swing your right leg up and over the horse's hindquarters."

As she lifted her leg, the horse took a small step forward. With her body halfway out of the saddle, she froze.

"Make sure your left foot stays put." Tyler's hand shifted to her waist, and he lightly gripped her to keep her from falling. "If you push it too much forward, Reba will think you're urging her to walk."

"Oh." Kinsey tried to move her left foot back, but the position was too awkward. She guessed she looked a little bit like a giant uncoordinated monkey trying to climb down a tree.

"Keep going." Tyler's voice was more encouraging than she'd expected. "I've got you."

She shifted her right leg again, and this time she managed to keep the horse from moving. As she brought her leg down, she clung to the saddle and the mane.

Through it all, Tyler's hand remained at her waist. Even though his hold was light, his fingertips seemed to sear through her shirt, making her skin suddenly hot.

As she planted her foot on the ground, he didn't let go. He was directly behind her, close enough that she could feel the power of his body.

"Now grab on to the pommel and slide your other foot out of the stirrup," he was saying.

She needed to focus on what she was doing so she didn't end up making a fool of herself. But as he settled his other hand onto her waist, she drew in a sharp breath at the contact. His hands were big and radiated strength. They were probably the kind of hands that could wrangle a steer or rope a bull. Tough. Just like him.

In the moment, however, he was handling her like a fine piece of crystal, as if she were delicate and breakable and something of value. Except that he didn't really value her. Yes, as a nurse. But beyond that, he didn't care about her.

As she tugged her left foot from its stirrup, she somehow managed to drop it to the ground without falling backward. A tiny misstep would cause her to collide with him, and she certainly didn't want that to happen. Didn't want him to think she was initiating something.

He'd already accused her once of trying to weasel her way into his family through Wyatt. So it was for the best if she didn't give him any other reasons to believe she was interested in him.

Even though she'd teased him about not finding a woman for a long while, there had been a few female staff members who'd come up to the house for one thing or another and had flirted with him. Today she'd seen him from time to time and noticed the way the female guests fawned over him. Then, of course, there was Nettie, the single mom that Tyler had apparently decided to pursue.

She wasn't right for him. That was obvious after just a few times of watching them interact when Nettie came to pick Wyatt up or drop him off. Nettie seemed nice enough, even pretty. But she was too docile, too accommodating, too simple for a man as forceful as Tyler

McQuaid. He'd walk all over her, and she would probably just let him.

However, the whole family was talking about the date he had with Nettie tomorrow night. They were so excited about it that she wouldn't be surprised if they were already planning the wedding. Even Wyatt had brought up that if his dad married Nettie, then Levi would become his brother.

Whatever the case, everyone thought it was past time for Tyler to start dating again, and they were glad he was making an effort, especially T.W.

"And that's how it's done." Tyler steadied her, his fingers tightening on her hips.

Was he leaving them there longer than normal? Or did it just seem longer because she was hyperaware of his touch?

"Thank you for your help." With his hands upon her and his presence boxing her in, a part of her wanted to stand there, maybe even lean back against him. There was something about him, about his masculine appeal, about his work-hardened body, about his rugged handsomeness.

Maybe she could understand to some degree why Nettie gushed over Tyler and treated him like a larger-than-life Greek god every time she was around him. Because he had a magnetic appeal that was almost too strong for a mere mortal to resist.

"I'm sure next time you'll be able to do it by

yourself," Tyler was saying. "You seem like a natural."

She released a laugh. "Reba could make anyone look like a natural. What is she, like, a hundred years old?"

"Ten."

"Same thing in horse years."

"There's no such thing as horse years." His voice rumbled behind her and hinted at humor.

"Dogs are seven times a human age, so why not horses too?"

"Because that's a load of hogwash." Was he leaning in closer?

"And what exactly is hogwash, Tyler?"

"It's a saying we use to mean garbage." Were his fingers on her hips tightening? Was his breath brushing against her loose hair?

No. She was just getting carried away and imagining things. "A washed hog is actually clean. So how does it mean garbage?" She had to put a stop to her dismounting lesson before she ended up like Nettie and stroked Tyler's already-too-big ego.

Before Tyler could answer her silly question, she reached for the reins that were now dangling over Reba's mane. With the reins in hand, she stepped forward, forcing Tyler to release her. Her motion prompted Reba to move too, putting several feet between her and Tyler and allowing her to draw in a full breath again.

She led the horse to the ranch hand who was still

standing in the middle of the corral and had witnessed Tyler helping her dismount. Maybe the young man hadn't realized how charged the lesson had been. Except, from the wideness of his eyes, she suspected he had.

Without a word, she handed off the horse, spun on her heels, and left the corral without a single look back.

12

A sibling dinner at Cliffside. It had been a while since they'd had one—at least since before Dad's cancer diagnosis—and they were overdue.

Tyler straightened his tie as he approached the hostess. Behind her, the rustic dining room held an elegance that had won the ranch awards and made each meal an experience that guests raved about.

Dozens of twinkling lights lined the ceiling beams and provided a source of illumination along with the candles in crystal globes on each table. Fresh white peonies with eucalyptus graced each table that was covered in a white linen tablecloth. The gold silverware, gold-rimmed plates, and gold-rimmed goblets added to the beauty.

As if that weren't enough, the floor-to-ceiling windows overlooked a waterfall and the rushing river below, with a balcony just outside the windows for guests to relax on once dinner was over.

When Emberly had texted Tyler that afternoon to suggest it, he'd readily agreed. He'd already had plans with Wyatt for a horseback ride through the woods for their Friday evening activity, but they'd finished in plenty of time for the sibling dinner.

Even though Brock wouldn't be there, at least Dustin was home for the weekend. Four out of the five of them would be able to catch up and talk about Dad without him hearing what they were saying.

Tyler had already talked with Dustin last night after he'd arrived via helicopter. His brother was between clients and awaiting his next protection agent assignment, and he'd wanted to spend his free time with Dad, fearing it might be one of his last visits. Dustin had admitted he was afraid Dad hadn't beaten the cancer and that the chemotherapy wouldn't get what was left.

Whereas Kade always saw the cup as half full, Dustin always saw it as empty. Maybe there had once been a time when Dustin had been happy and his life promising. But something had happened to change him—something he never wanted to talk about.

"Good evening, Mr. McQuaid." The hostess flashed Tyler a bright smile and watched him too eagerly.

She was new, and he couldn't remember her name, but she was friendly and professional with the guests, which was all that really mattered.

She glanced through the dining room, which was

almost full with guests in their best attire for the Friday night dinner and dance. "The back corner table is ready for you."

"Thank you." He tugged at his coat lapels before making his way toward the table they always reserved for one of their sibling dinners. In the corner against the glass wall, they had a little more privacy.

As Tyler made his way through the dining room, he was stopped by several guests, just like he usually was anywhere he went on the ranch. He glanced at the corner table to toss his siblings an apologetic look. But instead of finding four people watching him, there was only one.

Kinsey. And she was stunning—so much so that he halted his stride, stopped talking mid-sentence, and stared at her.

She was sipping from a glass of wine and peering out the window, her face aglow from the candles on the table. An elegant and form-fitting dark-blue evening gown showed off her well-honed body, and her hair was pulled back into a French twist with loose strands framing her cheeks, exposing her neck and shoulders and displaying her sparkling necklace and matching earrings to great advantage.

She was easily the most beautiful woman in the room, easily the most beautiful in the state, maybe even the most beautiful in the country.

He stood in the middle of the dining room,

unmoving like a marble sculpture. He could feel even more attention from surrounding diners shifting his way. He needed to move, but the air in his lungs constricted, and he couldn't take his next breath. He could only stare at her, his heart racing crazily with keen need.

Need for what? For her?

He didn't want to feel attraction to Kinsey, but helping her dismount at the corral had only fueled the fire he needed to douse.

Earlier, when he'd arrived in the barn and noticed her taking a riding lesson, he'd watched...to make sure the ranch hand wasn't flirting with her. Then Wyatt had shown up and joined in offering advice, and Tyler hadn't been able to drag himself away from the cuteness of it all.

If only he'd walked away then. But no, he'd had to stay. When the ranch hand had offered to help with the dismounting, the thought of that young man putting his hands on Kinsey had riled Tyler more than he'd believed possible. He hadn't been able to stop himself from storming out into the corral faster than an angry bull.

Even though he'd known he needed to keep his hands to himself too, he'd decided that he was better than some randy cowboy who might not respect Kinsey the way she deserved.

All that had been good and well at the time. But clearly, he was letting his contact with her, the nearness, and her beauty all go to his head.

When Kinsey's gaze finally flickered toward him, he forced his feet forward.

Who had invited her to their sibling dinner? Her presence wouldn't be ideal if they wanted to speak honestly and openly about Dad and his care. But it was Kinsey's day off, and after how hard she'd worked, she deserved to enjoy one of the impressive meals served in the dining room.

With each step that drew him nearer, her eyes widened, almost as though she hadn't expected him. Emberly had been the one to set up the dinner, and maybe she hadn't clarified to Kinsey who would be present at the sibling dinner, although the word *sibling* seemed pretty self-explanatory.

As he pulled out a chair and sat down across from her, he had the urge to fidget with his tie and coat again. In his suit, he knew he was fine-looking, especially because he'd taken the time to trim his scruffy face and slick back his dark hair.

But clearly he wasn't appealing to Kinsey, because she turned her attention back to the window and resumed slowly sipping her wine. Either that, or she was still angry with him for his resistance to having her at the ranch as Dad's nurse.

He needed to man up and be the one to break the ice between them. Even if they'd gotten off to a rough start, that didn't mean they couldn't put that behind them and at least be friendly to each other.

"You look nice tonight." He said the first thing that came to his mind, something he'd say to his mom or Emberly. But once the words were out, they felt too intimate, and he wished he'd come up with a better line.

"Thank you." She didn't look at him and continued to gaze out the window.

He scrambled to find a topic that wasn't so personal. "It's a beautiful view, wouldn't you agree?"

"It's incredible. I love it." She seemed to relax in her chair. "I was just thinking that whoever planned for the restaurant to be here is brilliant."

"Thank you. That *brilliant* person was me."

Her gaze swung to him. The blue-green of her eyes and the full impact of her beauty hit him in the lungs and drove the air from him. With her hair twisted up, her face was even more slender, showing off the high angles of her cheeks. The dangling earrings seemed to tantalize him, so close to the smooth stretch of her neck.

"You planned the location of the restaurant?" Her voice held a note of surprise.

"The first year I moved back after graduation from college almost ten years ago."

"So there was another dining room before this one?"

For a short while he explained the original structure of the ranch and then the projects he'd instituted after he'd taken over. Of course, he hadn't been able to make all the renovations at once. But gradually, over the past ten years, he'd turned an upscale ranch into a luxury destination.

During their discussion, a waiter poured him wine and brought out his favorite appetizer—steak and blue cheese bruschetta. By the time the waiter came to take their order, Tyler glanced at his watch and realized an hour had passed. None of his siblings were in sight. Had he mixed up the time of their dinner?

He pulled out his phone to find that he'd missed texts from all three, each of them giving him an excuse for why they wouldn't be able to make it to dinner after all. After he'd already arrived and sat down.

How convenient of them.

They'd obviously set him up on this dinner date with Kinsey. In fact, he wouldn't be surprised if his dad was the mastermind behind it since he liked Kinsey so much.

With a scowl, Tyler stuffed his phone away.

"What's wrong?" Kinsey paused in perusing the one-page menu, the waiter having stepped away to give them a few moments more while they waited for the rest of his family, who'd never planned to be there in the first place.

"Everyone else cancelled the dinner plans."

"I didn't realize Emberly had invited anyone else."

"She told you the dinner was with her?"

Kinsey nodded.

"And she told me we were having one of our sibling dinners."

"So…?"

"Which means Dad is playing matchmaker again."

"No…" She glanced at the empty chairs at the table, at him, and then down at her fancy gown. This time when she lifted her gaze, her cheeks had some pink in them. "I had no idea. I was just waiting for Emberly when you showed up."

"And I was waiting for all my siblings."

"Believe me, Tyler. I had nothing to do with this and didn't know anything about it."

He reached out a hand and touched her arm, hoping to reassure her. "I would never blame you for this."

"Why would T.W. do this?" Her brow furrowed. "We told him we don't like each other."

"Maybe he wants us to work on being friends?"

"Don't worry." She started to push back from the table and stand. "I'll set T.W. straight."

With his hand still on her arm, he latched on. "Wait."

She halted halfway up, her eyes flashing with determination.

He'd actually been having a nice time and wasn't ready for the evening to end. It wouldn't hurt to have dinner with her, would it? At the very least, he'd make his dad happy, and that was really all that mattered. "Since we're here, we may as well eat."

She hesitated, not standing but also not sitting back down. "I don't want to impose, Tyler. You were expecting to have dinner with your siblings, not your dad's nurse."

"You were expecting Emberly and not your patient's bossy son."

A smile hovered on her lips. Had he seen her smile yet? Maybe small ones directed at his son. But she'd never given him a smile.

"C'mon," he said softly and in his most convincing voice. "The chef here is out of this world. I guarantee you'll love the food."

She lowered herself back to her chair and picked up her menu. "What do you recommend?"

He breathed out a tight breath. Was he relieved that she wasn't leaving and he'd get to spend the evening with her?

That was ridiculous. He wasn't happy about being ditched by his siblings. He'd been looking forward to talking to them.

Yet he'd be lying to himself if he denied the thrill that was coursing through his veins at the prospect of spending more time with Kinsey.

A voice at the back of his head shouted at him that he shouldn't do it, that he'd sworn off beautiful women, that he didn't want to be attracted to someone like his ex-wife again. But as his gaze slid back to Kinsey, he couldn't stop himself from quietly closing the door on the warning.

Just one night with her. That was all he'd take. Then he'd go out on his date with Nettie and forget all about Kinsey.

13

She was having dinner with Tyler. How was that even possible when they barely tolerated each other most of the time?

Kinsey took the last bite of the rosemary potatoes that had come with the filet mignon. Tyler hadn't been wrong about the food. It had been one of the best meals she'd ever eaten. His company during the meal had been surprisingly pleasant too.

She'd enjoyed learning more about the history of the ranch, going all the way back to the original founder— Tyler's great-great-great-grandfather, Wyatt McQuaid, who'd claimed the land through the Homestead Act and built the first log cabin on the property back in 1862.

Tyler had explained how every oldest son had been named Wyatt, Tyler, or T.W. since then and how each had played a role in the expansion and development of the ranch over the years.

While the ranch had always done well with raising cattle and with the inn connected to the hot springs, the discovery of oil on the property in the mid-1900s had allowed for the more extravagant expansions that had finally put the resort on the map.

She'd especially liked hearing all that Tyler had done for the ranch since taking over as manager. He'd been innovative and savvy and hard-working, and from what she'd witnessed over the past week and a half, he was still just as hard-working. Even though he was in charge, he was constantly out and about the ranch, helping with anything that needed doing, including mucking out stalls, adding air to a bicycle tire, repairing a leaky sink in one of the cabins, and more.

Tyler was the kind of manager who led by example. He was never too busy or proud to do anything. He was personable with the guests and made them each feel like they mattered. Even throughout dinner, he'd paused eating to converse with anyone who passed by the table to greet him.

She could grudgingly admit Tyler wasn't as awful as she'd originally thought. After talking with him and learning more about him during the evening, she could even concede that he was a decent guy and easy to talk to.

Not only had he shared about himself, but he'd also shown a genuine interest in learning about her. He'd asked her about her work as a traveling nurse, what she'd done before taking the job with Premier, and even about her family. She wasn't ready to share the painful parts about losing Madison and her parents' divorce, so she'd kept to the basics like she did for most people.

"Did you save room for dessert?" he asked as he laid his napkin across his plate.

She wiped her mouth and then set her napkin on her plate too, taking the etiquette cues from him. She couldn't remember the last time she'd eaten in a place so fancy—maybe the time Madison had insisted on taking her out for her birthday. They'd gotten their hair and nails done, dressed up, and splurged on an exorbitant dinner in one of downtown Chicago's classy restaurants. Not long after that, Madison had told her about the terminal diagnosis.

Tyler sat back in his chair, his features relaxed, the usual stiffness gone from his posture. "The desserts here are to die for."

"I can't fit another bite into this dress." She pressed a hand against her stomach and the silky material of the dress that Emberly had insisted she borrow for the evening.

He swept his gaze over her stomach before slowly perusing upward. In the low lighting of the restaurant, his eyes were dark, but something smoldered in them—something she easily recognized as desire.

She'd seen it often enough in her life to know. And

she'd seen it often enough that she usually ignored it and let it pass her by. But tonight…it wasn't passing her by. His presence nearby was too strong, his good looks too charming, his eyes too intense for her to shake herself loose from that desire.

Instead, her insides fluttered like butterfly wings. The sensation was one she hadn't felt in a long time, and she wasn't sure what to do about it.

As his dark gaze lingered on her collarbones and then on the base of her neck, her breath stuck in her chest. She needed to say something light to break the growing charged tension, but she couldn't think of anything except for how incredible he looked at the moment, how incredible he'd looked all night in his dark suit. He was like a rich piece of chocolate silk cake, delicious enough to be on the dessert menu and eaten right up.

As if he'd heard her scandalous thought, his gaze lifted and collided with hers. His eyes had turned a shade darker. As his thick lashes lowered halfway, he didn't back down, didn't apologize for staring, didn't make any excuses for the blatant desire in his eyes.

The flutters inside fanned faster, sending warmth through her veins. She was tempted to press her hands to her cheeks to cool them down. But she also didn't want Tyler to know just how much his barest look was undoing her tonight.

Live music had been playing for most of the night,

and the lead singer began talking and inviting guests to dance.

Thankfully, Tyler broke his intense stare and glanced in the direction of the band and the dance floor.

She reached for her ice water and took a sip, letting the coolness seep into her overheated blood.

What was wrong with her? Why was she having such a strong reaction to Tyler tonight? Maybe it had been a mistake to agree to stay for dinner. Maybe it was blurring professional lines. After all, Premier had a no-intimate-involvement-with-patients policy. Tyler technically wasn't her patient, but he was close enough.

She pushed back and rose from her spot. "I should get going."

"No." He was on his feet in the next instant too. "Don't go yet."

She hesitated. She secretly liked that he didn't want her to leave. Even so, she had to put an end to the evening while the sparks between them could still be stomped out. "It's getting late, and I really should head back to T.W."

"You texted him thirty minutes ago, and he said he's doing fine."

She had been keeping close tabs on T.W. all day, checking in with him at least once an hour, even though he'd said she didn't need to. But she'd told him she'd have more fun if she wasn't worrying all day.

"You can't leave without trying dessert." Tyler's voice was earnest. "Which means you'll have to dance for a while to make room for it."

Couples were beginning to make their way onto the dance floor, but she'd never been much of a dancer. "I can't—"

"I won't take no for an answer." He held out a hand.

"Technically that wasn't a *no*. It was a *can't*."

"I won't take *can't* for an answer either." His outstretched hand didn't budge. If anything, at his full height and with his broad shoulders, he held himself with an intimidating self-assurance she wasn't sure she could resist—didn't want to resist.

How long had it been since she'd felt this way about a man? She honestly couldn't remember, as it had been years since she'd gone out on a date.

Was that what this was? A date?

She stared at his strong hand, his tanned skin, and his blunt nails.

"Just a few dances." His voice dropped low. "I promise that's all."

A few dances? She could do that. Then she'd say goodnight and walk away.

She placed her hand in his.

A smile curved up the corners of his mouth, turning him from handsome to slay-me-now gorgeous. She stopped breathing, stopped thinking, stopped moving and could only stare at that smile, half cocked and revealing perfect teeth. She most definitely needed resuscitation. But before she could call for it, his fingers tightened around hers, and then he was tugging her along behind him as he wound his way to the dance floor.

He didn't stop until they were in the middle, and then he slid one hand to her back and lifted their joined hands together.

She tried to focus on the dance, what everyone around them was doing, so that she could imitate the steps. But her every thought zeroed in on his hands. The one holding hers was firm and already guiding her in the moves of the dance, while the one on her back was tender and as light as a caress.

"I'm not a good dancer, Tyler."

"Lucky for you, I am." He smiled again. And the smile slayed her again too.

She was helpless to do anything but follow his lead as he moved proficiently around the dance floor, guiding her and twirling her with an ease that helped her to relax. She found herself catching on in no time and was soon enjoying the dancing more than she'd anticipated.

When the band finally paused for a break, she was breathless and hot and happy. Still holding her hand after the past hour, Tyler tugged her along again, this time toward a glass door that led to the balcony overlooking the waterfall and river.

Darkness had already descended, but several lights placed strategically along the river and waterfall illuminated the sparkling, cascading droplets, turning them silver in the moonlight.

Other couples had come out onto the balcony too, having the same idea as Tyler to cool off and enjoy the view.

Tyler led her to a more secluded end of the balcony. Only when they were standing at the railing side by side did he release his hold on her hand. For an irrational second, she was tempted to grab it back, wasn't ready to lose the connection with him.

She grasped the wrought iron instead. What was she thinking? That after growing familiar with his touch and hand during the dancing, she could go around holding his hand whenever she wanted?

He leaned his forearms on the railing and peered out at the view.

She sneaked a peek his way, his chiseled outline making her heart skip irregularly. After being in his arms and dancing face-to-face, she figured she would have had her fill of him. But maybe he was the kind of man a woman craved more rather than less.

She really had to get a grip on herself. She didn't want to crave more of Tyler. Not only would craving him be entirely unprofessional, but they also didn't get along. Or at least they hadn't gotten along until tonight. Now she couldn't remember what about him she'd disliked.

Regardless of these strange new feelings, she wasn't in a place in her life where she wanted a relationship—casual or otherwise. Not when she was still intent on building her career.

Besides, her traveling schedule didn't allow for dating. After she finished one job, there was always another waiting for her. If she had a day or two—or sometimes three—between positions, she went to visit her mom in Naperville, since she'd long ago decided to give up her apartment. There was no sense in keeping something so permanent when she was gone ninety percent of the time.

There was also no sense in getting involved with a man when she had such a nomadic lifestyle. She didn't have room in her life for a long-distance relationship, and the logistics would be a nightmare. So why bother starting one at all?

Yes, Tyler was in the market for a wife to bring his dad happiness and health. And T.W.'s brush with death had obviously made him realize he wanted to see all his children happily married before his time on earth was over.

However, their newfound goal to find Tyler a wife wasn't her problem. Not that Tyler would consider her a viable candidate for a wife anyway. They might be feeling some chemistry tonight—okay, maybe a lot of chemistry—but it didn't mean anything. He had to know as well as she did that whatever was sparking between them was temporary. Very temporary.

"You're a good dancer." Tyler finally broke their silence.

She bumped her shoulder against his. "And you're a good liar."

Her sarcasm earned her another smile, a wide one that showed a flash of his teeth and brought out crinkles at the corners of his eyes.

Her breath hitched. Ugh. Why did his smiles have to make him look so roguishly charming?

She couldn't think about that. "You must have done a lot of dancing when you were growing up."

"We had lots of good, old-fashioned barn dances back in the olden days."

"Back in the olden days." She scoffed. "Like fifteen years ago when you were in high school?"

He shrugged. "Barn dances, cow tipping, and tractor races. What else was a rowdy high-school guy supposed to do up here in the high country?"

She tried to picture Tyler being rowdy and couldn't imagine it. "I bet you were chasing girls."

"Guess I did my fair share of that too."

"Is that when you met Stephanie?"

At the mention of his ex-wife's name, he stiffened. She'd only heard a little about Stephanie from T.W., and most of it had been positive because that was just the way

T.W. was. He probably didn't want to criticize Stephanie, especially in front of Wyatt.

"T.W. told me she's really sweet to Wyatt."

"When she's around." Tyler's voice held a note of bitterness.

Kinsey waited for him to say more, but he let the silence stretch so that the cheerful conversations of the other guests filled the space.

She could admit she'd been curious about the woman who had won Tyler's heart. But it wasn't her place to pry, and in the long run, it didn't really matter who Tyler had once loved. "I'm sorry for bringing her up."

"It's all right."

"Clearly it's not."

He blew out a taut breath. "It's past time to move on."

She'd told that to her mom more times than she could count, especially when it came to Madison's room, which remained unchanged.

Maybe Mom's inability to move on was why Kinsey liked moving on—to prove she wasn't stuck in the past the same way her mom and dad were.

Tyler stared off into the dark distance beyond the waterfall. "Stephanie was a beautiful woman, and I was crazy about her. But beyond the attraction we felt for each other, we had little else in common."

A beautiful woman he was crazy about? A strange

jealousy pinched Kinsey, although she wasn't sure why. Tyler didn't mean anything to her.

"She came up here for me and had lots of ideas for the ranch." This time Tyler's voice held a note of something else. Was it regret? "But it didn't take her long to realize she didn't enjoy the ranch lifestyle and being away from the fast pace of a big city."

"So she didn't grow up here?"

"She was from New York City. We met in college."

"I spent several weeks in New York City earlier in the year on a job there. It's a whole other world." But it hadn't bothered her, since she was from the Chicago area and used to big-city life.

Tyler was silent for several long heartbeats. "I know my dad wants me to get remarried...but..."

"You want to be careful to find someone who isn't intimidated by the West?"

"Exactly."

"I'm sure plenty of women would enjoy living on your ranch and having this in their backyard." She nodded at the waterfall.

He sighed heavily. "I'm not taking any chances next time."

"That makes sense." If she were in his situation, she'd be careful too.

"That's why I'm looking for someone who's from the area."

"Ah, that's why you're going out with Nettie even though she's all wrong for you."

Tyler shifted so that he was leaning on one elbow on the railing and facing her.

Was he mad at her now? If so, they would be back on familiar ground. She glanced at him sideways.

He was watching her but didn't seem mad. Instead, his mouth was starting to quirk up on one side. "Who made you the expert on who's right or wrong for me?"

"It doesn't take an *expert* to know."

"Oh really?"

"I haven't known you long, and already I've got you figured out."

Tyler leaned back on his elbow more comfortably, as though he was settling in for a conversation that he intended to relish. "Since you have me figured out, why don't you tell me the kind of woman you think I need."

She shifted so that she was leaning on one elbow now too. She pretended to study him. "Hmmm...you definitely need someone who won't run and hide every time the grizzly bear comes out."

"The grizzly bear doesn't come out much."

She raised her brows.

"Maybe it comes out around you more than normal, but that's just because you poke it until it does."

"I poke it?"

"Yes, you know how to push my buttons."

"True."

He ducked his head and fought back a grin. "What else do you think I need in a wife, oh wise one?"

"Oh wise one? You got that right." She liked that they could banter easily.

"So?" he persisted.

"You need a woman who has a backbone and can stand up to you with her own needs. She has to be independent and have her own life so that yours doesn't swallow her up."

"And...?"

"And..." Her thoughts spun with all the qualities that a complicated man like Tyler would require in a wife. "Maybe she needs to be a little feisty to keep things from being too boring."

He didn't respond. Instead his eyes rounded her face, taking her in, caressing her even though he wasn't touching her. The dark brown smoldered again, clearly communicating he liked what he saw. And that he'd like to do much more than just look at her.

The fluttering in her stomach from earlier returned, twisting and turning inside and making her almost dizzy with a strange wanting.

"It sounds like you're describing yourself," he whispered as his gaze touched on her mouth.

Had she been describing herself as his ideal wife? "No, of course not."

He arched a brow.

Maybe she had accidentally projected herself, but she hadn't meant to. "I admit. You would have the perfect woman if you did find someone like me. In fact, she'd be awesome."

"Awesome?"

"Completely and totally wonderful."

"Are you offering yourself as a candidate?" Even though his tone held a note of teasing, his eyes contained a seriousness that surprised her. He wasn't serious, was he? Hadn't he just said he wanted someone who was local, who was used to the high country, who wouldn't get tired of the wilderness life the same way his ex had?

She shifted to look at the river, trying to formulate the right response. "I know you want to make your dad happy by getting married, but you can't sacrifice your happiness in the process. And if you marry the wrong woman, that's what you'll be doing."

He was quiet for several long moments. "If I can save my dad, then any sacrifices I may have to make will be worth it."

How could she argue with that? She would have done just about anything to save Madison, even sacrificed her own happiness if it had meant Madison would have lived.

"I understand," she whispered, the gravity of the moment weighing upon her.

She could feel him watching her, could sense his dark

eyes probing, trying to see deeper inside her. But she didn't like talking about Madison, especially all that had happened during her last year.

She forced a smile. "As much as you'd like to consider me as your top wifely candidate, I'm afraid you'll have to satisfy yourself with just friendship."

He hesitated. "I'd like friendship, Kinsey."

The sincerity in his tone drew her gaze.

He was watching her with serious eyes, the smolder gone, the sparks extinguished. "I'd like that much better than being enemies."

Her smile relaxed. "Me too."

14

"I win." Kinsey laid her last card, a jack of diamonds, on the bedside table.

Tyler watched her face, waiting for her smug smile. As it spread across her lips, warmth speared his chest the way it had been lately whenever she smiled—smugly, sweetly, or any shape.

"You're cheating." Tyler fake scowled and then tossed down his last few cards, pretending to be disappointed, but he'd never been more content.

Kinsey flopped back in her chair next to Dad's hospital bed. "I'm just better and smarter, and you know it."

"Not better or smarter than me."

From the bed, Dad snorted. He was resting peacefully, his head elevated, his eyes closed, his breaths even. Now he cracked open one eye, his look warning Tyler to be nice to Kinsey.

Tyler didn't need the warning. Over the past two weeks since the dinner with her at the Cliffside restaurant, their relationship had settled into a comfortable friendship. With Wyatt in New York City, Tyler had been able to spend more time with his dad in the early mornings and evenings. He'd also had more time for card games, talking, and watching crime shows.

Of course, it was a bonus that Kinsey was in the room most of the time and that she joined in the games, talking, and show-watching.

"I thought you were sleeping." Tyler rose and resituated his dad's pillow behind his head. If he'd known Dad was awake, he would have invited him to play Kings in the Corner with them.

"It's hard to sleep with the two of you going at it." Dad's voice held distinct pleasure.

This time Tyler was the one to shoot a warning glare. His dad needed to tame his enthusiasm for the matchmaking. Tyler had repeatedly insisted that he and Kinsey were just friends and that was all they'd ever be. But Dad hadn't gotten the message. Or if he had, he'd chosen to ignore it.

Dad closed his eyes and settled back into the hospital bed.

Tyler didn't let up his glare, hoping his dad could feel it even if he couldn't see it. Things with Kinsey were

146

good, and Tyler didn't want anything or anyone to ruffle their friendship.

Because the truth was, he liked their friendship, and he liked her. Not just because she was beautiful. Yes, every time he saw her, he admired how stunning she was. Every time he saw her, she made his heart race faster. But he was learning to keep his attraction shuttered away where it belonged so there wouldn't be any wayward sparks that ignited and caused flames.

She was a friend. Just a friend. Those words were on repeat inside his head, and now they replayed again. "I can't help it if Kinsey likes to cheat." He lobbed out the comment again, knowing full well she never cheated. She was just competitive and smart and savvy. And she was playful and fun.

Not only did he enjoy spending time with her, but he also liked how easy she was to talk to. When they weren't talking about Dad or what was happening on the ranch, they talked about everything else—childhood stories, high school and college experiences, and places they'd both traveled—she'd definitely been to more places.

She'd opened up a little about her family, sharing about a sister who had died four years ago and how her parents had given up on their marriage of thirty years. He'd sensed the hurt the topic still caused her and hadn't pushed her to say more than she'd wanted to, which hadn't been much.

He'd enjoyed telling her more about his siblings, because he was so proud of each of them and how hard they worked. None of them were perfect and each had their own struggles, but he loved them. At least once a day, Emberly and Kade came by the house to see Dad and check on his progress, and it was clear the two of them both liked Kinsey too.

Whatever the case, the camaraderie with Kinsey was one of the best parts of his day, something he was starting to look forward to more than he should.

Whenever he worried about his feelings toward her escalating, he reminded himself that her time at the ranch would soon be drawing to a close. She'd been there for almost one month, and Dad was getting stronger with each passing day. The incisions from his surgery were healing well. He was regaining an appetite and had actually sat down at the table for a meal last night. He was getting around the house more, and over the past few days, Kinsey had taken him for short walks outside.

Kinsey had indicated that Dad could possibly be strong enough for chemotherapy in two or three weeks. By that point, Dad wouldn't require a full-time nurse any longer. If he needed any help at all, Kinsey had suggested they look for a home health aide or certified nursing assistant who could visit every day.

When both he and Dad had offered to keep paying her to stay, she'd laughed and told them that as much as she'd enjoyed her time at the ranch, she wasn't paid the big bucks to babysit. She wanted to go where she would be needed.

Tyler understood what she was saying. Or at least he was trying to. She'd said that she loved being able to help people, and once she finished with Dad, she wanted to move on to the next complicated case and bring hope and healing to someone new.

"Go ahead and deal again," Dad said as he sat forward and began to press the buttons of his hospital bed. "I'll play the next hand and make sure Kinsey doesn't cheat anymore."

Kinsey smiled warmly at Dad. "You know I never cheat with you. I only do it with Tyler because he cheats too."

Tyler scoffed and began to gather the cards.

Kinsey stood and took the cards from him. "Hand them over or you're going to be late for your date."

Tyler paused and glanced at his watch. In the next instant, he jumped up from his chair. "Shoot. I'm already late."

Kinsey continued to collect the stray cards from the table. "I'm sure Nettie won't mind. You could tell her you're flying out to lasso the moon, and she'd tell you that's a grand idea."

He'd already gone out on one date with Nettie the night after the dinner and dance with Kinsey. He'd taken

Nettie to a local restaurant in Healing Springs, and they'd had a nice time. Nettie had been nice. The food had been nice. And the evening had been nice.

Nice.

He was satisfied with nice. Nice was all he needed. He didn't want the fireworks that had been going off inside him during his dinner and dance with Kinsey. Those fireworks had been hot and exciting and even pleasurable, but he only had to think back to the fireworks that he'd had with Stephanie to remind himself that the spectacular colors and the dazzling lights fizzled out eventually, leaving only ashes.

"Nettie wants to take me to the VFW for their Friday night fish fry."

"The VFW?" Kinsey's bright blue-green eyes fixed upon him and filled with a hundred questions, and not just about what a VFW was.

"The American Legion."

Her brow just quirked higher.

"It's a club for veterans, and they serve food."

"Oh." Her one-word answer said everything, particularly that she still didn't think Nettie was right for him.

"It'll be fine." He'd been trying to convince himself of that all week after Nettie had suggested the VFW for dinner and shopping at an antique store afterward. "I'm sure no matter what we do, it will be fun." At least, that's what he was hoping for. It wasn't necessarily about what they did but that they were together and getting to know each other.

"You're right." His dad sat forward and swung his legs over the edge of the bed. "You go have fun with Nettie, and I'll keep Kinsey company tonight."

Kinsey laughed lightly as she moved to Dad's side. She wasn't helping transfer him anymore, but she did position herself close by in such a way that, most of the time, Dad didn't even realize she was hovering.

Dad rose and Kinsey pretended to keep shuffling the cards as she stayed by his side. She was very good at what she did. That had become abundantly clear over the weeks of watching her work.

Tyler inwardly cringed at how judgmental he'd been the first couple of weeks. He'd been a donkey. Not many women would have put up with his chauvinism and shown him as much grace as she had.

Kinsey Wingrove was a classy woman. That's all there was to it.

He needed to find a way to officially apologize and say thank you before she left the ranch. But how?

"Go on now," Dad said with a wave of his hand. "Enjoy your night. Who knows? Maybe you'll fall in love with Nettie tonight, and we'll have a wedding to celebrate soon."

Dad smiled at him, but there was something knowing

in his dad's expression, as if he understood what Tyler really wanted was to stay and keep playing cards with Kinsey.

He'd set his dad straight after the night of the dinner and dance with Kinsey when he'd learned that his dad had indeed been the one to convince Emberly and Kade and Dustin to cancel their plans. Tyler had confronted his dad the next day and asked him not to do any more matchmaking and had explained that he and Kinsey had agreed upon being friends, but that was as far as either of them was willing to go.

Thankfully, his dad hadn't pushed them together again and had respected the boundaries Tyler had set in place.

Tyler crossed to the door and hesitated there. Was there a part of him that wished Dad would push a little harder to get him and Kinsey together? Maybe so.

But doing so was futile. Kinsey wasn't interested in him in that way. She'd made that clear enough. He couldn't let himself become too interested in her either. She was from Chicago, another big city, and didn't fit into the ranch or country living. She was used to going everywhere and doing everything and seeing the country. She'd already worked in thirty states for her traveling nurse job, and she had the goal of traveling to the final twenty.

With a short sigh, Tyler exited his dad's room and

forced himself to focus on the date ahead with Nettie. She deserved his full attention, not a half-hearted effort at dating. It wouldn't be fair to either of them if he let thoughts of Kinsey occupy his mind.

The June evening was hot, and the VFW wasn't air conditioned. Neither was the antique store. By the time they'd finished strolling through the musty rooms, Tyler was hot and tired and ready for the date to be over.

When Nettie suggested getting ice cream to cool off, indicating that Levi's grandmother wasn't expecting her home for another hour, Tyler went with her to an outdoor ice cream stand where she ordered Levi's favorite ice cream—blue moon—by mistake. Her lips and tongue turned bright blue, embarrassing her enough that she called it a night. Thankfully, she was in a hurry to go inside, and as he walked her to the door, he wasn't faced with the choice of whether to kiss her goodnight or not.

It was relatively early when he returned to the ranch. The night sky still reflected the setting sun, and the warmth of the day lingered. A low-voltage restless energy hummed through him. He stopped by his office in the lodge and worked for a little while. Then he swung by the barn and checked on the foals. Even there, the restlessness lingered.

He tried to ignore it, tried to pin it on missing Wyatt, but as he headed up the hill toward home, the anticipation swelling in his veins wouldn't allow him to ignore or deny the truth—that he wanted to see and spend time with Kinsey again.

As he entered the house, he made his way directly to his dad's room. He knew that was where she stayed for most of the night, dozing in the bedside chair and only going to her room and sleeping in her bed once she knew Dad was in a deep sleep. Even now, with Dad doing better, she still kept long hours, wanting to be there just in case Dad needed anything.

Tyler admired her dedication, but he also wished she didn't push herself so hard. He knew she did it because she took her job seriously and because she truly cared about her patients. But a part of him wondered if her unwavering determination stemmed in part from her desire to atone for losing her sister. Kinsey hadn't talked much about Madison, but he'd gleaned enough to know the death had been difficult.

With a bounce to his step, he entered his dad's room. He searched first for her, his gaze landing upon the bedside chair where she was curled up, her legs tucked up and head resting against the wing of the chair. She was asleep, her pretty face relaxed, her long lashes resting against her cheeks.

Dad was watching the news with Mom asleep in the crook of his arm. At the sight of Tyler, he pressed a finger against his lips and cocked his head toward Kinsey, warning Tyler not to wake her up.

"I'll carry her to bed," he whispered.

Dad nodded. "She works too hard and needs another day off."

"Then give her one."

"I've tried. But she won't take it."

Tyler bent over Kinsey, positioning himself for the best angle to scoop her up without waking her.

"Maybe if she had something to do on her day off," Dad whispered, "and someone to spend it with."

"Emberly could do it again."

"I was thinking you could."

Tyler straightened and leveled a stern look at his dad. "Don't start playing matchmaker again."

"You need a day off too."

Tyler just shook his head. "I'm already seeing someone."

"You went out on a couple of dates with Nettie. That doesn't mean you're a couple yet."

"Nettie thinks we're getting there."

"And what do you think?"

He shrugged. "I don't know."

"Then spend the day with Kinsey and decide after that."

Tyler's whole body hummed with even more energy at the prospect of being with Kinsey for an entire day. "What makes you think Kinsey would agree to spend her day off with me?"

"Plan something, then give her no choice." His dad's eyes held a challenge that dared Tyler to figure out a way to win Kinsey over.

Tyler hesitated. Did he want to win Kinsey over? No, he didn't. But now that his dad had planted the idea of spending hours with her, he wanted that more than anything else.

Could he find a fun activity, or perhaps several?

His mind spun with a dozen ideas. He had the money and the means to do just about anything. Something special, something that would impress her, something that would make a memory that she could keep forever—maybe lots of little memories that she could take with her when she left the ranch.

Yes, tomorrow, he'd make Kinsey's day so special that she would never forget it or him.

He leaned down again and gently scooped her up so that he was cradling her.

She stirred, and her lashes flitted up halfway. Her hazy eyes locked in on his. "Hi. You're home." The words were warm and welcoming, as if she'd been waiting for him, which wasn't true at all.

He started to carry her across the room.

"I'm fine, Tyler," she said through a yawn. "Put me down."

He kept going.

Her lashes fell, and she let her head rest against his

shoulder. Her hair was tumbling from the messy bun she was wearing, and pieces tickled his chin and cheek.

Since her eyes were closed, he let himself look at her face and take in each exquisite detail for as long as he wanted, rarely having had the opportunity to stare and get his fill without her knowing.

Shoot. Why did she have such elegant beauty, the kind a man could look at every hour of every day and never get tired of?

He made his way carefully to her room next door. He pushed the door open with his foot, then crossed to her bed, which was unmade with clothing scattered over it. He lowered her gently while at the same time smoothing out the spot.

As her head sank into the pillow and he started to release her, her eyes fluttered open again, and her gaze connected with his in a drowsy way that sent a surge of heat along his veins.

"How was your date?" Her whisper was soft and sleepy.

"It was fine."

"*Fine* means it wasn't great."

"*Fine* means nothing went wrong and we had a nice time."

"*Nice* also means it wasn't great."

"*Nice* means I like her and will probably ask her out again." Maybe. Maybe not. He wasn't sure. But he wasn't admitting that to Kinsey.

Her lips curved into a small smile as she closed her eyes. "It's time to move on, Tyler."

Was it time to move on from Nettie?

His dad's diagnosis of cancer had made him realize how short life could be, that he didn't have time to waste on things that weren't important, that he needed to focus on what really mattered.

Why run after something—someone—he didn't want when what he wanted was right in front of him?

He shook his head and then spun away from Kinsey. They were just friends, and that was all they could ever be.

15

Kinsey stepped into T.W.'s room, the bright morning light coming through the windows blinding her.

As she squinted, a hand snaked around from behind and covered her eyes. "I'm kidnapping you for the day." Tyler's voice rumbled near her ear.

His brawny arms were boxing her in, and his thickly corded chest bumped into her from behind. His woodsy pine-and-cedar scent was strong, like it usually was in the mornings after he showered.

"Kidnapping?" She didn't resist him. She didn't want to, even though she knew she should.

"You're taking the day off," T.W. called from the bed.

"I'm watching T.W. all day," Leah chimed in.

"I didn't agree to this." Kinsey could picture the couple as they'd been last night, snuggled up together on the bed, their love so alive and so sweet. Instead of letting T.W.'s cancer tear them apart, they were letting it bring them closer. From the way everyone admired the couple, Kinsey guessed the two had worked at having a strong marriage all along—a marriage that could stand during the storms instead of crumbling.

"I knew you wouldn't agree. That's why I'm kidnapping you." Tyler kept his hold firmly over her eyes and then reached for her hand with his other one. His fingers rounded hers, grasping her firmly and giving her no option but to go along with whatever he was doing.

"What exactly do you intend to do with me?" She kept her voice light and tried not to think about all the ways he could answer that question.

"It's a surprise." His answer contained a thread of arrogance, but it sent a thrill through her anyway.

She was expecting him to take her around the ranch so that she could try more of the activities that guests got to experience—like white water rafting or the ropes course. But he had a Jeep packed with bags and said they had a drive ahead of them. When he asked if she wanted the top of the Jeep up or down, she rolled her eyes and told him that of course she wanted it down.

As they headed away from the ranch toward the west, the wind bathed her face, and Tyler blasted Brock's newest country music album. The beauty of the morning filled her soul with wonder, and every once in a while, Tyler pointed to something for her to look at—a herd of mustangs grazing, pronghorns lifting alert heads to watch them as they passed, and prairie dogs scurrying in and out of burrows.

When they reached the western range and started up the switchbacks, she was again awed by the majesty of the scenery. Tyler drove the roads with a confidence and skill that made it clear he'd grown up in the mountains and knew exactly where he was going.

He parked the Jeep in a small gravel lot, outfitted himself with a backpack, and then led her up a trail. They hiked for a mile or more until they reached an alpine lake that was so pristine and glassy it reflected the peaks surrounding it. With only a few other hikers lingering by the lake, she felt like she was in a little slice of heaven on earth.

Tyler spread out a blanket on a smooth rock at the water's edge and then proceeded to arrange a picnic lunch on it. She was famished and ate with a gusto that matched Tyler's. They finished off the sandwiches, chips, and fruit easily. Then they lay back on the rock and rested contentedly.

"Thank you, Tyler." The clouds floated in front of the sun, providing some shade. "This is the best date ever."

He cleared his throat. "So we're on a *date*?"

"No!" She sat up quickly. "Of course this isn't a date."

Except for a grin, he didn't move, remaining sprawled out and completely relaxed beside her with his eyes closed. "Seems to me you're protesting a little too much."

He looked so good. His light blue T-shirt with the ranch logo strained at his shoulders and around his arms. His muscular legs, tanned and fit, stretched out from long shorts. With a baseball cap and sunglasses, he'd shed the rugged-cowboy look and instead perfected the preppy-hiker vibe.

"We're just two friends on a hike together." She tossed out the words as casually as she could this time.

"Fine. Just two friends." His hand shifted and brushed against hers. The caress was light and feathery on her knuckles, but the impact of it smacked into her chest, making her suddenly breathless.

She needed to pull her hand out of reach. She had to abstain from any physical contact in order to keep the invisible fence up between them as she had the past two weeks since the night of the dinner and dance.

But as his finger traced a line from her knuckles to her wrist, her resistance crumbled just a little, and heat raced up her arm and shimmered across her skin.

What was he doing? And what did this picnic mean to him?

As if hearing her unasked question, he cracked open one eye and glanced up at her. "Ready to go?" He wasn't pulling his hand away from hers, was instead now drawing a circle on the back of her hand.

The circle sent a surge of desire through her. But a

desire for what? For him? For more of his touch?

She expelled a taut breath. She didn't want their time together to end. But she wouldn't be able to sit next to him a moment longer without saying or doing something she might regret later.

"I'm ready." She began to gather the containers from their lunch and return them to the backpack.

With a smug smile, he joined her, clearly realizing the impact of his touch upon her and enjoying that he was getting a reaction.

The hike back to the Jeep didn't take as long. She'd expected him to direct the vehicle back the way they'd come, but he drove the opposite direction. He didn't touch her again and moved the conversation to easy topics, almost as if he wanted to distract her.

By the time they arrived in a little mountain town called Frisco, the conversation between them was flowing again as naturally as it always did. They stopped and got ice cream, and then they walked around the little tourist shops while he insisted on buying her an expensive bracelet as a souvenir. He wouldn't take no for an answer, so she paid him back by getting matching Colorado ball caps and T-shirts that had huge gopher heads on them.

Wearing their identical gear, they drove a short distance to a large field where a hot-air balloon was waiting for them. The pilot was a McQuaid cousin, one of many who lived in the state. As they loaded up, the cousin teased Tyler about her, claiming that Tyler hadn't divulged he was bringing a lady friend along, especially one so beautiful...and in matching shirts and hats.

Tyler took the teasing good-naturedly, joking back with his cousin. Before long, the balloon with its brilliant stripes was rising up from the ground, floating steadily higher until miles and miles spread out around them.

She leaned against the basket, and Tyler stood beside her, pointing out various landmarks—the Blue River, the Dillon Reservoir, the Tenmile Range, and more. The view was incredible with the river valley nestled among the mountains covered in blankets of dark-green pine.

She'd never been in a hot-air balloon before, but with Tyler beside her and his cousin carrying on a commentary of Summit County and its history, she felt completely at ease and relaxed, just as she had at the alpine lake.

Tyler was proving himself to be as innovative and creative with their day together—not date—as he was with the activities at the ranch, and she could tell how much he was enjoying showing her Colorado. Was he hoping she would fall in love with the high country the way he had? If so, she was.

"I'd take another nursing job in Colorado in a heartbeat," she said once they were back in his Jeep and driving to a new destination that he wouldn't reveal.

"There's a medical office in Fairplay." Tyler's statement was casual, but there was also something strangely charged about it, as if he was fishing for information.

"Returning to routine wellness checks after years of caring for the most severely ill patients?" She tried to keep her tone light. "I'm not sure I would know what to do."

"I've also been thinking about adding a part-time nurse to our staff on the ranch."

As soon as the statement was out, she didn't know what to say. Was he indirectly trying to discover if she'd be open to staying in the area? She wasn't sure. But she did know she couldn't lead him on into thinking she was willing to settle down into a permanent position. Because she wasn't, was she?

He glanced at her sideways, then focused ahead again on the road. His profile in the waning evening light seemed harder and more chiseled than usual. Or maybe he was just more serious about this conversation than he had been about others.

Either way, she had to make certain he knew she wasn't interested in staying long-term. In fact, she'd just talked to Pippa a few days ago about potential new assignments.

"I've even thought about building an ER in Healing Springs," Tyler continued. "That way we have something closer and don't have to medi-flight every serious case to Frisco or Colorado Springs."

"Sounds like a good idea."

"Does it?" His question held a note of hope.

"With as many tourists as the area draws, it seems like a practical addition."

"But…?"

"But what?"

He glanced at her again sideways. "You don't seem enthusiastic about the idea."

"No, I am. It seems great."

He was silent for a beat. "Just not great for you?"

She sighed softly, feeling as though her answer might let him down, and she didn't want to do that. And yet she had to be honest. "I haven't lived anywhere permanently in four years because of all my traveling."

"Don't you ever get tired of it? Of always moving and never having a place to put down roots?"

She shrugged. "I know it's probably hard to understand, especially for a man whose roots run two centuries deep. But I like moving and meeting new people and having new experiences."

He was silent for several long heartbeats before nodding. "You're good at what you do, Kinsey. I'm sorry I ever doubted you."

"Thank you. I'm glad we turned things around and can be friends."

"Me too."

She waited for a reassuring smile from him, something to relieve the pressure that was mounting between them. But nothing came.

She was tempted to ask him what was going on and what he was feeling. A part of her knew the conversation was far from over, that it was just beginning. But she was too afraid to keep going down the path they'd begun, too afraid of what he'd say, too afraid of where it might lead.

They were better off sticking to what they currently had and keeping their relationship uncomplicated and fun.

As if recognizing the same, Tyler blew out a breath and then changed the subject, turning their conversation to more lighthearted topics again. When they arrived at an exclusive mountaintop restaurant, Tyler handed her a bag that Emberly had packed with a change of clothing for the evening—an elegant silver gown and blingy shoes and jewelry.

Tyler changed too, and took her to the best table in the establishment, with a rooftop view of the sunset while they ate. The food was almost as good as Cliffside Dining Room, but they both agreed the Healing Springs chef was superior. They stayed to listen to the live music afterward, but when she started yawning, he cut short their night amidst her protests, and they started back toward the ranch.

She dozed for part of the way, the full day of sunshine, fresh air, and activity having worn her out. As they entered through the gate and it clanked shut and locked behind them, she yawned and stretched.

"I couldn't have asked for a better day off. Thank you."

He was relaxed in his seat, one hand on the wheel. "I'm glad I got to be the one to show you more of the state."

"I'm glad you were the one too." And she meant it. Just because she didn't want to be in a serious relationship with him didn't mean she couldn't admit just how much she'd enjoyed his company today.

He drove the Jeep slowly. Was he reluctant for their day to come to an end?

It was late, and from what she could tell, most of the guests were back in their cabins. She'd already been in touch with T.W. and Leah, and both had assured her there was no hurry for her to return. Leah was staying with T.W., and all was well.

The problem-free day was just one more indication that T.W. was improving and wouldn't need her much longer. In fact, Kinsey suspected she could take another job sooner than she'd expected.

For tonight, however, she didn't want to think about leaving. She wanted to enjoy the end of a really fun day without ruining the mood.

She stretched, then winced. "I thought I'd be in better shape than I am, but I'm feeling that hike."

Tyler tapped his thumbs against the steering wheel for

a moment, then veered the Jeep toward the lodge. "I know just what you need."

"You do?"

"Yes."

"More ice cream?"

"Something even better."

"I doubt anything could be better than ice cream."

"Trust me. There is."

He drove the Jeep around to a parking lot near the lodge. He was at her door before she could open it all the way, helping her down. She'd discarded the heels Emberly had packed for her and now her feet were bare.

"What are we doing here?" She peered at the elegant lodge, some of the windows still lit, but most were dark since the hour was late.

"You'll see." His feet crunched against the gravel as he started in the opposite direction of the lodge.

She took several steps, the rocks biting into her soles. "Hold up. Let me grab my shoes."

He halted. In the darkness that was lit by a full moon overhead, he looked more darkly handsome than ever, his suit now unbuttoned and his tie hanging loosely. "What happened to your shoes?"

"I took them off during the ride." She pivoted and began to make her way gingerly back to the Jeep.

Before she could protest, he was hoisting her off her feet and into his arms.

She released a small yelp. "What are you doing?"

"What does it look like?" He started forward with his long stride, easily carrying her.

"I can walk, you know." But she honestly didn't mind. She'd been half asleep last night when he'd carried her to her bedroom, and she'd liked both the gentleness and strength he'd displayed when he'd deposited her on the bed.

He was already moving out of the parking lot to a wide mulch-covered trail. The waft of his cologne was faint but still tantalizing, and the warmth of his body seemed to welcome her to lose herself in his arms.

Maybe it was a bad idea to head out for another adventure with him tonight. After spending the day with him, she needed to put some distance between them and keep him firmly in the friend zone.

However, as she rested her head against his shoulder, she couldn't find the strength to tell him no. Besides, he was stalking forward with such purpose and intensity that she didn't have the heart to dampen his enthusiasm.

The other truth, which she didn't want to admit even to herself, was that she liked the feel of his sculpted body, the hardness of his chest, and the heat of his arms. His breathing echoed near her ear and against her cheek, tickling her in the best possible way and sending tingles down her arms.

When he stepped off the wooded trail and into a

clearing, he came to a halt.

She glanced around to find what looked like a gated pool area and an elegant pool house. From the sulfur scent lingering in the air, she knew where they were. The hot springs.

16

Tyler didn't want to put Kinsey down, but he had to in order to open the locked gate that led to the hot springs. Besides, now that the paths were paved and smooth and kept perfectly clean, he had no excuse for holding her.

Reluctantly, he lowered her to the ground.

She stepped forward and peered through the gate. "I didn't realize the hot springs were open at night."

"Technically, the area is closed."

"Then what are we doing here?"

"We're using the pools anyway." He pulled out his master key card. "One of the perks of being the owner."

"I take it this isn't the first time you've snuck in here."

"Definitely not." He swiped his card, and the gate clicked open. He stepped aside and waved her ahead of him.

She hesitated. "Is this where you take all your women at the end of your dates?"

Was there a note of jealousy in her voice? "I thought you said this wasn't a date."

"It's not. Absolutely not."

"Then does it matter?"

"I just don't want you thinking you can bring me here and…you know."

"No, I don't know. Illuminate me."

She snorted, then moved past him, her pretty silver gown shimmering in the moonlight and reflecting against her hair, which was loose, the brown soft with highlights. He hadn't been able to stop admiring the long strands since she'd met him in the restaurant dining room after changing clothing.

He closed the gate and stood beside her as she took it all in. The solar-powered ground lights around the hot spring and other pools glowed all night. The underwater lights in the pools illuminated the crystal-clear water along with the stone interiors. The paths that wound through the various levels of pools were also made of stone, the same color and patterns as those inside the pools, but larger. Everything, including the landscaping, was elegant and intended to wow the guests.

Was it wowing her? He hoped so.

"So," he probed. "What is it you think I do with my dates when I bring them to the hot spring at the end of the night?"

"Tyler McQuaid." Her voice sounded scandalized,

and she padded quickly down a path—the wrong path.

He lunged forward and grasped her arm, bringing her to a halt.

With a hitch of her breath, she swung around, her eyes wide and luminous and her lips parted. What had given her the impression he was a womanizer?

His gaze dropped to her mouth, to those open lips, so pretty, so sassy, so perfect. Suddenly the thought of kissing Kinsey was right there at the front of his mind.

"Did you bring Nettie out here last night?" Kinsey whispered.

He couldn't keep a smile from creeping out. "You're jealous."

She clamped her lips closed, glared at him, then spun and started walking again. "No, I'm not."

He grasped her arm again.

When she halted, this time she turned and looked directly at his mouth, as though she believed that the reason he'd stopped her so abruptly was because he intended to kiss her. He'd stopped her so that he could lead her down the adjacent path, to the bathhouse where she could change into a swimsuit.

His smile curved higher. Yes, she definitely had kissing on her mind. Thankfully, he wasn't the only one.

"So, how many women have you kissed out here?" she whispered, still watching his mouth.

He leaned closer, unable to stop himself from teasing

her just a little. "A few."

"Give me a number."

"Three."

"You've kissed three women here?"

He shrugged. "It was a long time ago in high school."

"So you didn't kiss Nettie here last night?"

He liked the jealousy in her tone. Liked it a lot.

The fact was, he liked *her* a lot, even more so after the day he'd spent with her. There hadn't been a moment when he'd thought about the ranch or work or Wyatt or even Dad. He'd been focused on her and only her because she was so vibrant and full of life. She'd been fun and energetic and had embraced every single one of his activities enthusiastically, filling him with a satisfaction he'd never known before. He didn't understand it. All he knew was that he'd loved making her happy, and he'd loved being with her when she was happy.

He also loved that she was being possessive of him. And that she didn't like the idea of him kissing other women. That had to mean something, didn't it?

He angled in so that his mouth was only inches from hers. Although he was still teasing her, the closeness was all too real, her warmth too near, and her body too beautiful to ignore.

Shoot. He really wanted to kiss her, wanted to see if her lips tasted as good as they looked. He had the feeling that a woman as independent and strong as Kinsey wouldn't be a passive participant in kissing, that she'd be just as independent and strong in her kissing.

His heart began to race faster. Could he just bend in and take one kiss? There wouldn't be anything wrong with that, would there?

"Well?" She lifted her hands and pushed at his chest, forcing him to back up a step. Her eyes were slanted and demanded an answer.

What had they been talking about?

Kinsey's expression remained expectant. She wanted to know about Nettie and kissing.

"No. I haven't brought any women out here in years, not even Stephanie."

The confession seemed to placate her, because a smile tugged at her lips. "Not that it matters or anything."

"Of course it doesn't matter." He couldn't stop himself from reaching for her hand and enfolding it in his. He didn't give her the chance to pull away, and instead, began to tug her along behind him toward the right path.

The expertly manicured gardens that lined the pools were brimming with blooming flowers, the heady scent lingering in the air. Stone benches were strategically placed along the paths. A covered patio with tables and chairs surrounded a large hot tub built into the ground. Another area led to a full heated pool with deck chairs for guests to relax in the sun.

A luxurious bathhouse and a snack bar bordered the pool. As he unlocked the door and led her inside, he opened the gift shop and told her to pick out a swimsuit. She browsed for a few moments, then found the plainest swimsuit on the rack—one that was made for serious lap swimming, not a late-night rendezvous.

Not that he wanted her to pick something pretty. She was already attractive enough. But she clearly thought he had ulterior motives in coming to the hot springs and was picking a swimsuit she thought would deter him.

"Listen, Kinsey." He pushed away from the store doorway where he'd been waiting. "I didn't bring you here to seduce you or make out or whatever you think I'm planning to do."

"I know."

"Then what?"

She hesitated, twisting at the tag on the swimsuit. "I'm making sure we keep our relationship where it needs to be."

"And where's that?"

"In the friend zone."

Her words doused the sparks that had been flaring to life all day. The truth was, it had been a spectacular day. He'd enjoyed every moment, from riding in the Jeep with the top down to belting country music songs together to talking about anything and everything. Yes, the special activities he'd planned had been amazing too. But her presence had been the only thing that mattered.

Had he been hoping she would be feeling more for him by this point? Because he couldn't deny he was feeling more for her. He hadn't stopped to analyze how much more and what that meant, but it certainly went beyond the *friend zone.*

He'd even brought up the various nursing jobs in the area, trying to gauge whether she'd be open to something besides traveling nursing. He'd been hoping she might be having the same tug toward him and, as a result, might consider a more permanent position.

But he should have realized when she'd told him she liked traveling that she was keeping him as just a friend, like she was doing now.

If he were honest with himself, he knew that was for the best, even if it was disappointing. He was getting too caught up in his attraction to her...and he was forgetting all the reasons why he needed to be careful about letting his attraction get the best of him. Mainly so that he didn't repeat the mistakes he'd made with Stephanie.

Yes, Kinsey was different from his ex in a lot of ways. Stephanie had always been too optimistic, too bubbly, and too carefree. She'd thought love was all it would take for them to make their marriage work. When the reality of life and hardships and difficulties had fallen upon them like they did for every married couple, she'd been disillusioned.

Kinsey wasn't like that. She was realistic, practical, and responsible. She handled hardships and difficulties every day in her work. And she'd experienced loss already in her own life with the death of her sister. In spite of all the challenges, she was strong and kind and compassionate—more than most people he knew.

Even if Kinsey wasn't like Stephanie in some ways, there were still too many similarities that scared him—namely that Kinsey wasn't used to living outside a big city. She would eventually get tired of a rural ranch the same way Stephanie had.

He held up his hands in surrender. "I'm stepping back into the friend zone."

Kinsey quirked a brow at him. "It's that easy?"

"Yep." No, it actually wasn't. He couldn't just turn off the attraction he was feeling for her. But he didn't want to let it overrule solid reasoning the way he had when he'd been dating Stephanie.

Kinsey pulled a white bikini off the rack and held it up. "So, my *friend*, you'd be okay if I wore this instead?"

His mind filled with an image of her wearing the flimsy covering—a sizzling image that dumped gasoline onto the sparks inside him. The flames sprang up high and fast and hot. Rapidly, before they could consume him, he stomped them out.

As if she could sense the firefighting battle inside him, her lips tilted up with a sassy smile.

"I'm not a saint, Kinsey," he growled.

"So the blue Speedo?" She held up the plain suit she'd taken off the rack first.

"Fine." He turned and began to stalk toward the changing rooms, wishing he weren't so weak. Because the truth was, he didn't want to lust over her. He wanted to respect her and their friendship.

Friendship with Kinsey. That was all he could ever have. And that was all he needed. If only he could convince himself of it.

17

Kinsey groaned with pleasure as the shallow warm water of the hot spring enveloped her. It was silky smooth, like the finest cotton sheet, wrapping around her, tangling her up, and tingling through her skin.

At the splash of water, she opened her eyes to find that Tyler was moving away from her to the opposite side of the pool. His bare back faced her in all its expansive tanned glory.

As he sank into the new spot and turned, she got a perfect view of his chest, which rivaled his back with its muscular grandeur. His pecs and abs were like the granite mountain peaks she'd seen earlier in the day—rock solid, with chiseled lines and smoothly rounded curves. She couldn't deny that she wanted to run her hands over his shoulders and down his arms and feel all that solidness beneath her fingertips.

The thought was completely unwanted but sent

shimmers of heat through her belly anyway. He was already too easy to look at with all his clothes on, much less wearing only swim trunks.

She shifted her gaze down to her legs stretching out in the water, the low lights showing off her toned muscles. She couldn't let herself think about Tyler's body. Not now, after she'd made a point of clarifying with him that they were only friends and that nothing but friend-ness was going to happen tonight in this gorgeous place that was entirely too romantic.

He was staring down at his hands under the surface of the water, his expression tight, almost pained.

"What's wrong?" she asked.

"Nothing." The one word was clipped and different from how talkative he'd been most of the day, even from moments ago after they'd changed. He'd grabbed them both bottles of lemonade from the snack bar, and then, on the short walk to the original hot spring that had been on the property when his family had first lived on the land, he'd explained how they'd expanded the hot springs over the years and tapped into a deeper underground source to create several other smaller pools known for their varying temperature levels.

She didn't understand all the science behind the hot springs, but she understood that people from all over came to experience them because of the healing myths associated with the water.

The original Ute Natives of Colorado had been the first to discover and use the hot springs, making claims about their healing properties. Apparently, miraculous healings had taken place over the years as a result of the hot springs. Family members who'd had ailments had been cured or nearly so because of the water. There were also stories of guests who had found relief from sicknesses.

T.W. hadn't come to the hot springs since his cancer diagnosis, but Tyler had considered bringing him over, although he'd admitted he didn't believe sitting in the healing springs would actually heal cancer.

Kinsey didn't discount prayer and miracles. She also believed homeopathic remedies as well as complementary and alternative medicine had a place once in a while. But as a registered nurse, she was trained to address physical problems with modern medicine and treatments that were scientifically proven to be helpful.

Regardless, she loved when Tyler talked about the things he was passionate about. He was interesting and knowledgeable, and she liked seeing him come to life.

But there were also times when his moods turned more somber. Sometimes that happened when he was thinking about his dad, although not as much recently since T.W. was improving. Sometimes that happened when conversations steered in the direction of his ex-wife. Sometimes that happened when he considered his family and the challenges each of his siblings faced.

She appreciated that Tyler was a deeply caring man who took his responsibilities seriously. But he also needed someone in his life who could listen to him and be there and share some of his burdens so that they didn't all fall so heavily on him.

As a friend, she could be that person for him, couldn't she?

"What are you thinking about?" she asked softly as she leaned back against the smooth stones that made up the side of the hot spring.

He sank down into the water, submerging his body up to his shoulders. Even though he was across from her now, the pool wasn't huge, and his outstretched leg and foot bumped against hers.

"You're so serious all of a sudden," she said.

"Sorry." He tilted his head back and looked up at the dark sky that sparkled with a million stars.

Here in the high country, the sky seemed close enough to reach up and touch. At night, especially, the stars hung just a little lower and sparkled just a little brighter.

"Don't be sorry."

He was silent for several heartbeats, then expelled a sigh. "The blue Speedo isn't helping."

A strange heat shot straight through her abdomen.

"But don't worry," he continued. "I'll stay on my side over here and won't cross the line."

The heat spread through her body. It had been so long since she'd allowed herself to spend time with a man like this.

"You should know," she said lightly, wanting to make him feel more at ease, "it's hard to avoid looking at you too."

"Is that right?" His tone lost some of the tightness.

"You already know you're eye candy."

He huffed a laugh.

"Or maybe I'm just getting old and losing some of my ability to resist a handsome man."

"So I'm handsome?"

"Oh, please."

He smiled, obviously satisfied with her roundabout compliment. "You're not getting old."

She shrugged. "Twenty-eight isn't young anymore."

He was quiet for a moment. "How long have you been in resistance mode?"

"Resistance mode?"

"When was your last serious boyfriend?"

"I haven't had one in a long time."

"See? Resistance mode."

She skimmed the surface of the water with her hand, letting the silk flow through her fingers even as the memories flowed through her mind. "My last boyfriend was when I was in college. Christian."

Tyler was quiet, eyes on her, waiting for her to tell him more.

"He was a basketball player, one of the best on the team." She'd met him in the gym while working out their sophomore year, and they'd started dating a few months after that. "We were both busy. He traveled a lot with the team, and I was taking hard nursing classes and was studying all the time."

"But you liked him?"

"I think I loved him." She couldn't keep her tone from growing wistful. He'd been a good guy, super sweet and caring, even if he'd been obsessed with his basketball career.

"What happened?" Tyler's voice was soft but held an intensity that told her he wanted to know everything, that he didn't want her to hold back any longer.

She liked when Tyler shared with her. Maybe she needed to consider being vulnerable with him in return. It was what friends did.

Still, she hadn't opened up to anyone in a long time. Only Pippa.

"You don't have to say anything—"

"Near the end of my senior year, we discovered Madison had acute myeloid leukemia. So I broke up with Christian because I didn't want to be distracted in helping to take care of her."

"That must have been hard."

"Christian took it better than I expected, probably because he'd already made plans to play professional

186

basketball in the Euroleague."

Tyler's scowl fell into place. "So he let you go without a fight?"

"I don't blame him at all. I let him go without a fight too."

"He didn't ever contact you again?"

"We met up a few times when he came home on breaks, but I was too distracted by everything going on with Madison and had nothing left to give him. Eventually we fell out of contact. Last I heard a couple of years ago, he got married."

Tyler studied her face, his expression gentling. "He's a jerk for giving you up and for not being there with you."

She sighed. "We had a battle ahead with Madison, and I didn't want to ask him to walk through that with me."

"The right man would be willing to walk through anything with you."

"Maybe. But Madison had already struggled with other health issues over the years, so I knew the work would be intense if we had any hope she'd make it."

Kinsey could admit that Madison's many childhood illnesses had been part of the reason why she'd chosen to go into nursing. She'd always wanted to find more ways she could help, always wanted to be the one by her sister's side.

"Madison was determined to beat the leukemia,"

Kinsey continued. "She stayed in school for months, even though she was sick and nauseous and fatigued most of the time."

"She sounds like a brave young woman." Tyler's statement was heavy with compassion.

A lump rose swiftly into Kinsey's throat, but she pushed past it. "Watching her waste away and knowing there was nothing I could do was the hardest thing I've ever gone through." Her voice wobbled in spite of her effort to keep it steady.

He sat up and shifted forward as though he intended to cross to her and offer her comfort. But then he stopped and held himself back, a man of his word, unwilling to cross the invisible line that he'd drawn in the pool.

The need for his comfort rose swiftly within her. She'd never gotten that from Christian, since he'd walked out of her life the way she'd asked him to. She'd certainly never gotten it from her parents, because they'd been too busy fighting over Madison. Of course, Pippa had been there during Madison's last year, offering encouragement and support. But that had been in the form of pep talks about staying strong and pushing forward.

Kinsey had been strong and had pushed forward. She'd done it for Madison, who'd told her not to give up and to live life for them both.

Now, with Tyler watching her so intently and so compassionately, she wanted to simply lay her head on his shoulder and let him hold her. In fact, her body suddenly ached with the need for someone to lean on who cared about how she felt.

Without giving herself a chance to second-guess her decision, she glided across the water toward him. As if sensing her need, he stood and opened his arms. In the next moment, he was embracing her, his arms surrounding her, his body cushioning her.

She slid her arms around him too, letting his solidness seep into her.

She closed her eyes, unable to keep the sorrow from welling up—sorrow that she'd stuffed down for so long that she hadn't even known how much it all still hurt.

Tears squeezed out along with a shudder—or maybe a sob.

His arms tightened around her.

This was what she hadn't known she needed— someone who would just hug her and let her cry. She'd been so alone and had to be so strong on her own for too long. Now, with Tyler's comfort and silent support, she wanted what he was offering so keenly that she wasn't sure how she'd gone so long without it.

More tears fell onto his already slick chest, sorrow for all she'd once had and all she'd lost—the happy childhood, the happy family, the happy future together. It was all gone. So was the ideal dream where she and Madison both had husbands and families of their own and came home to spend time with Mom and Dad, who loved each other and waited at the front door with their arms around each other and welcomed them back.

Kinsey wasn't sure how long she stood in the pool in Tyler's arms. But eventually the chill of the night breeze brushed against the upper half of her body, which was out of the water.

She sniffled, her cheek resting against Tyler's chest. She released the stiffness of her body and relaxed against him. "Thank you, Tyler," she whispered.

"Anytime," he whispered back.

That same longing from before rushed in. What would it be like to have someone strong and steady to lean on like this during the troubles life brought? Because there would be more troubles. She'd been a nurse long enough and had seen enough tragedy to know that life on this earth was broken and not everything could be fixed. That wouldn't happen until heaven, where a better place waited.

In the meantime, what if she'd been missing out on having someone to hold hands with during the difficult journey? Maybe that was the whole point of having that special someone—because together, they could navigate the troubles better and keep each other from falling when they stumbled.

Tyler was resting his chin on her head and had both arms locked around her back.

She knew she shouldn't think about Tyler as a possibility for that special someone. Not when she'd been so adamant they were just friends. But in this moment, with his comfort so sweet and so freely given, a swirl of desire began to pulse through her.

She needed to pull back and put space between them, but she loved the closeness and loved being supported in a way that she couldn't remember ever feeling before.

"If I were Christian," Tyler murmured, "I wouldn't have left you."

"It was my fault—"

"It doesn't matter. You needed him, and he walked out of your life."

She pulled back a little, wanting to see Tyler's face.

He released her and took a step away.

The warm water swirled around her, caressing her skin. But without him holding her, she felt cold and alone and wanted to be back in his arms.

He took a larger step backward, clearly putting himself squarely on his side of the pool and into the friend zone. He didn't intend to take advantage of their proximity or her moment of sorrow. Instead, he was respecting the boundaries she'd set.

A sweet pleasure cascaded through her as she watched him retreat to the stone wall, where he lowered himself and stretched his arms out along the wall. He was as darkly handsome wet as he was dry. The pool lights only added to his rugged, almost fierce appeal, showing every sinew and ripple of his muscles in his arms and chest.

This man was one of the kindest, most giving, and most thoughtful men she'd ever met. He truly cared enough about her that, even though he'd been fighting against an attraction to her that he'd openly admitted to having, he'd released her and wasn't pursuing his own needs.

In fact, from the way he'd latched on to the edge of the pool tightly with both hands, he seemed to be holding himself back. He was also keeping his gaze trained on the water and avoiding checking her out.

Oh, honestly, how could she resist a man like him? And why was she so set against it? What harm could come from giving in to their attraction to each other and seeing where things might lead? Yes, it would probably be complicated with her traveling. But if they cared enough about each other, they could find a way to make a relationship work, couldn't they?

No, he hadn't exactly come right out and said he wanted a relationship. But he'd been hinting at it from time to time today.

She took a hesitant step toward him.

His gaze shot to her face, revealing stormy eyes.

She shivered and moved another step closer.

His jaw flexed as though he wanted to say something, but he held himself back.

Slowly, she glided through the water, until at last, she was standing in front of him.

He hadn't taken his gaze from her face. His eyes were still brewing with a storm, and his expression remained hard and rigid. His arms were taut, and his grip on the pool caused his biceps to bulge and the veins in his forearms to pop.

The desire for him that she'd been denying and locking away came marching out, needing to be set free. She lowered herself in the water so that she hovered in front of him. Then she extended her arms until she was grasping both of his shoulders.

His gaze skimmed her arms before darting back to her face.

She boldly circled one of her hands behind his neck and swam even closer to him so that she was now only inches away.

He held himself absolutely motionless. "What are you doing, Kinsey?" His voice was low and hoarse.

"What does it look like?" she whispered.

"It looks like you crossed out of the friend zone."

"It looks that way to me too." She dug her fingers into his neck.

"You don't have to." This time his gaze dropped to her mouth and stayed there.

"I want to." She tugged his head forward, and at the same time, leaned in so that her lips collided with his. She didn't waste any time with a polite, soft prelude. Instead, she moved against him forcefully and hungrily. Because she was hungry for him after the past days and even weeks of denying her attraction. It had languished inside her, growing more famished by the day so that now she couldn't get enough of him.

He wasn't tentative in his response either. His arms snaked around her, drew her flush, and his mouth devoured hers in return. The tempo was fast and hard and desperate. Almost as if they both knew the kissing was forbidden and that they had to feast as much as they could before the meal ended.

She didn't want it to be forbidden, didn't want him to be off-limits. But what had changed between them? Yes, he'd listened to her and helped bear the weight of her grief, but the obstacles between them hadn't changed.

His hands slid up her back under the water. His fingers were taut against her skin and his hold was possessive.

The feel of his possession ignited more sparks inside her, incinerating the objections that were prodding at her. She angled in and meshed her mouth with his again and again, tasting him and wanting to possess him too.

For long minutes she felt like she was back in the hot-air balloon, where the world belonged to only them, where they were the only two who existed, and where they could live in a bubble of euphoria forever.

But at the intensity of the kissing, her breathing grew ragged and so did his, until finally he released a groan and pulled his mouth away and rested his head against hers. His grip was tight, his body rigid, his chest heaving. Hers was the same, and she couldn't move, could only lean against him.

She'd never kissed anyone like that before and doubted she ever would again. The simple truth was that Tyler McQuaid was hands down the best kisser in the world. If she died right now, she'd die knowing she'd had the best kiss of her life.

He shifted, and his chest brushed against her—a very bare, very hard, and very broad chest.

He was half naked, she wasn't exactly decent either, and they were alone in a pool at night. The combination was only asking for trouble, especially with the heated pleasure that was burning a trail through her body.

What was she doing anyway?

All the objections she'd been attempting to silence came rushing back with double the force. She was leaving soon. She didn't have any permanence to her life. More importantly, she'd made it her life mission to help people like Madison who needed a nurse who understood their suffering. She couldn't just give that up, could she?

An unbidden fear prickled along her nerves. She released her hold of Tyler and stood.

Although he seemed reluctant to let go of her, his

arms fell away, almost as if he sensed the change in her emotions.

She began to cross toward the stairs and could feel his gaze trailing her. She didn't want to leave him, but she also knew she couldn't stay.

18

Tyler couldn't tear his gaze from Kinsey as she stepped out of the hot spring. His blood was still overheated, his breathing uneven, and his body decimated. Kissing her had weakened him to the point that he wasn't sure he could stand and make his legs hold him up.

Even as he took in her beautiful body, her curves, and those endless long legs, much more than physical desire pulsed through him—so much more it was overwhelming. The power of his feelings filled his chest and made it swell with an ache he didn't understand, something he'd never experienced before.

All he knew was that he'd do anything for her, that he'd even die for her if necessary. He didn't want to be apart from her ever again, hadn't wanted to let go of her and let her walk away, wanted to chase after her and spend every second with her for the rest of his life.

Was he in love with her? Was this the passion that his

dad had tried to explain, the McQuaid legacy of love, the one the McQuaid men were known for? The deep, abiding, and consuming love each McQuaid man experienced when he found the woman who completed him and made him into a better man?

Tyler had the feeling that was exactly what this was and that he'd finally found the love of his life, the one his dad had been praying he'd find. The feeling was scary and exhilarating at the same time, and he didn't know what to do about it.

A part of him wanted to race after Kinsey, tug her back into his arms, and kiss her until she could feel his love. Another part of him wanted to blurt it out, tell her how hard he'd fallen for her and how he didn't want to live without her, not for a single day.

She'd crossed to where they'd set their towels and phones, and she started wrapping her towel around her body. Her back was stiff, and she hadn't looked back at him yet. She was also too quiet, which meant she probably regretted her rash decision to leave the friend zone behind and make a move toward more.

He could admit he'd been surprised when she'd glided across the pool toward him, the glow in her eyes telling him that she was interested in him as more than a friend. But he'd waited, hadn't wanted to initiate anything, hadn't wanted to pressure her in any way.

Should he have put on the brakes? At the very least,

should he have tamed his response? Maybe he should have kissed her softly and then hugged her again?

But he wasn't sure he could have restrained himself more than he had. Already, he was anticipating the next kiss with her, the next chance to hug her, the next chance to have her close. It was almost as if he wouldn't be complete until she was back by his side.

Was that how it was for his dad? Why Dad was truly only content when Mom was with him, sitting beside him and holding his hand. Did he feel that a piece of him was missing without her?

Although Tyler had desired Stephanie, he'd never had this overwhelming need for her or this sense of completion with her the way he did with Kinsey.

Kinsey picked up her phone and glanced at the screen. Immediately her expression changed. She swiped and began to read a text.

He tensed and rose. "What is it?"

"T.W. He's throwing up and having a lot of pain."

Tyler lunged to the edge of the pool. "What's going on?"

She was already calling someone and held up a finger toward him. "Leah?" She paused and listened, but the soft hum of the pool prevented him from hearing his mom's voice on the other end of the phone. "Yes, that's good. You're doing the right thing."

Tyler climbed out quickly. His pulse thudded hard,

but he tried to calm it. Dad was improving. Kinsey was here. They would figure out this new complication together. It couldn't be serious.

"Just get there as fast as you can," Kinsey said firmly but calmly, the tone she used often when she was in her nursing role. She listened to his mom for a few more seconds, then nodded. "We'll meet you there."

As she ended the call, she turned to face him, her expression grave.

He didn't bother grabbing the other towel. Instead, he reached for his phone to see he'd missed phone calls and texts. Two from his mom. One from Emberly. And several from Kade. From an hour ago.

"An hour?" His voice rose with disbelief. Had they really been away from their phones for an hour in the hot spring? As with the rest of the day, he'd lost track of time while he was with Kinsey. She'd been all that had mattered. He hadn't been able to think of anyone or anything else and had been in a world where only the two of them existed.

She moved toward the path that would take them back to the bathhouse. "They're on their way to Penrose Hospital. Kade's flying them."

Falling into step beside her, Tyler's heart dropped. "It's that serious?"

She lengthened her stride. "I don't know, but they

didn't know what else to do since they couldn't get ahold of me."

His mind raced with the possibilities, including the chance that the cancer was back and growing and that they were too late for chemotherapy. "What do you think is wrong?"

"I don't know without being able to assess him."

"What were his symptoms?" he persisted.

"Just what I've told you—that he was in a lot of pain and throwing up."

"What could that mean? That the cancer is back?"

They were practically jogging now. "There are lots of things it could mean, and we won't know until we get some scans."

"How much time until they reach the hospital?"

"They just left."

"Why did they wait so long to leave?"

"They were hoping to get advice from me." Her tone was terse.

"We should have been paying better attention to our phones." His voice was escalating too, along with his tension, but he couldn't stop his frustration, mainly aimed at himself for not being available, for not checking his phone sooner, for getting so distracted with Kinsey.

She didn't respond. They had reached the bathhouse, and she could hardly make it in fast enough. They hurried through their changing. He hustled out of the men's room, in the shorts and T-shirt he'd worn earlier in the day for their hike, and she'd changed into her shorts and T-shirt too.

He didn't bother going to the house. Instead, he directed the Jeep toward the mountain pass that would take them to Colorado Springs. The drive was usually over an hour, depending on the traffic near Pike's Peak. Thankfully, at the late hour, they didn't have that to worry about. Even so, there was no way to speed up traveling the mountain passes.

They spent the majority of the drive on the phone talking to his mom and siblings. By the time they reached the hospital parking lot, it was close to midnight, and they were even more on edge.

They rushed into the ER and found everyone in the private waiting room they'd used earlier in May when they'd brought Dad to the hospital for the first time. Kinsey wasted no time in tracking down a nurse, explaining who she was, and then getting an official update. She learned that his pain was under control, and they were doing all kinds of testing.

No one would say what everyone was thinking—that the cancer had multiplied and spread and was causing the pain again. Kinsey asked the nurse to order more tests that would detect complications from pancreatic cancer including diabetes, insufficiency of pancreatic enzymes, or an obstruction.

As they sat together in the waiting room, Kinsey kept busy checking with the ER staff and doctors. She was also on the phone with her agency and one of the doctors from the Mayo Clinic in Rochester who was on duty at the early morning hour. She held his mom's hand and talked with her for a while. Then she called another specialist and ordered more tests.

Tyler's own worry kept him pacing the waiting room just as it had the last time they'd been here. Once again, he felt as though he didn't know what to do or how to help anyone.

When the doctor finally came into the waiting room, they learned that Dad had an obstruction in the duodenum of the small intestine and that in the morning, he would have surgery to insert a stent to keep the area open. The doctor assured them it was a common occurrence for those suffering from pancreatic cancer but also very treatable.

They drank lots of coffee throughout the morning as they waited while Dad was in surgery. When they finally got the news that the procedure was done and had been successful, they rested more easily. Kade spread out on one of the couches in the surgical waiting area and promptly fell asleep. Emberly offered to drive the Jeep back to the ranch so that Tyler could ride back with Kade in the helicopter. And Mom was allowed to go to Dad's bedside and sit with him.

Tyler only caught glimpses of Kinsey from time to time as she continued to advocate for Dad's care, demanding only the best. He was glad she was so strong and knowledgeable and helpful. But as the morning passed into the afternoon, he missed being with her more than he wanted to admit.

Finally, as she stepped into the waiting area with box lunches for him and Kade, he stood and reached for her hand the way he'd wanted to all night and all morning. He just hadn't been ready to make his feelings for her public, especially around his family, and especially at a time like this.

"Sit with me," he whispered, casting a glance at Kade to make sure he was asleep.

His brother was still sprawled out, his arm draped across his eyes.

Just the touch of her fingers against his set his insides on fire, and the sight of her in front of him eased the ache in his chest. At some point she'd changed into scrubs and pulled her hair up into a messy bun. Even with a crinkled forehead and dark circles under her eyes, she was gorgeous.

He'd noticed the way the doctors and other male staff looked at her every time she was near. Their eyes followed her and lit with appreciation at not only her beauty but her engaging personality. She was friendly and personable while being direct about what she wanted, and she was able to get her way with most things because of it.

Regardless, his muscles had stiffened every time he'd seen her talking to another man, and he'd wanted to go over and claim her, maybe even put a sign on her that said she belonged to him.

Except that she didn't belong to him. At least, not yet.

He wasn't sure exactly how to move forward with her, wasn't sure of anything at this point...except that he knew without a doubt that he loved her and wanted her.

"I can't sit, Tyler." She tugged her hand loose and took a step back.

"You have to eat too."

"I'm not hungry." There was something in her eyes. Sorrow? Frustration? Fear?

He didn't know what it was, but it set him on edge. "At least rest for a little bit."

"I will later, once T.W. is awake and I know he's okay."

Tyler glanced around to gauge his level of privacy. Kade hadn't moved. No one else was nearby.

Tyler closed the distance between them and this time touched her chin lightly. "I miss you."

She didn't move except to lift her eyes up to him. The blue-green was the color of a forest of blue spruce and just as vast. For a moment, they were wide open and revealed her feelings for him—at least, he thought he was seeing a softening of affection there.

But she shook her head and lowered her gaze, shuttering her eyes with her long lashes. "I've got to go, Tyler."

Then before he could stop her, she spun and wove through the chairs, out of his reach. He fought against the urge to chase after her and find out what was wrong, because something wasn't right.

When she disappeared past the doors of the surgical recovery unit, he expelled a taut breath, then plopped into his chair.

Lying on the adjacent couch, Kade raised the bent arm that was covering his eyes. He peered at Tyler with a smug smile. "I knew it. You've got the hots for Kinsey."

Tyler glared at his youngest brother, feeling like he was back in high school and Kade was still in elementary school. Being nine years younger, Kade had been a pest when it'd come to the girls Tyler had brought around to the ranch, always teasing and making a big deal out of Tyler's dating life. Obviously Kade was still a pest.

"I don't have the *hots*, Kade." Tyler didn't care that his tone was slightly superior or irritated. "I like and respect Kinsey. There's a difference."

Kade rested his arm on his forehead and continued to peer at Tyler with a growing grin. "I could see the sparks flying between the two of you from day one."

Tyler rolled his eyes as he picked up one of the to-go

boxes Kinsey had given him.

"It's just a matter of time before you kiss her." Kade's voice was much too confident.

In the process of opening his box, Tyler paused. He hadn't had much time to think about the kiss he'd shared with her in the hot spring. Now, at just the brief remembrance of it, heat shot through his gut, and his muscles tightened with need.

Eyes widening, Kade pushed up to his elbows. "You already kissed her."

"It's none of your business." Tyler hastily continued unpacking the contents of the to-go box.

"And it was more than just a kiss." Kade's voice took on a note of excitement. "It was the knowing kiss."

"What do you mean 'the knowing kiss'?"

"It was the kiss that confirmed she's your one woman, the love of your life."

"I didn't need a kiss to figure it out."

"So she is your one." Kade said it with so much confidence that Tyler could almost believe his brother was right, that Kinsey Wingrove was his one.

The desire for her swelled so swiftly and keenly that Tyler pressed a hand to his heart. It wasn't physical desire as much as it was the need to be with her, sit beside her, talk with her, look into her eyes, see her smile, and hear her laugh. It was all he wanted to do. In fact, if he did that forever, he'd be satisfied.

Tyler sat back in his seat and nearly rolled his eyes at his own sappy self.

Shoot. He had it bad for Kinsey. He was helplessly and hopelessly in love with her.

19

She was leaving the ranch and taking a new job tomorrow.

Only one more day to avoid Tyler. Only one more day to keep up her façade that everything was okay when it was anything but okay. Only one more day until she left and could start mending her aching heart.

With the early-morning sunshine slipping through the slits in the curtains, the June day promised to be sunny and warm and as beautiful as so many of the other days she'd experienced over the past month.

Kinsey gave T.W. another sip of ice water, then started lowering the head of his bed. "There you are. Why don't you see if you can go back to sleep for a little while."

He nodded wearily, his eyes already closed.

After two days in the hospital in Colorado Springs, he'd returned yesterday afternoon by ambulance. She'd ridden by his side the entire way while Leah and Tyler flew back in the helicopter.

Even though T.W was weak and tired after the pain and the surgery, he was in good spirits as always. Since getting home, Leah had been inseparable from him and had only just left the bedroom to take a shower and get ready for the day.

And Tyler…

Kinsey's chest squeezed at the thought of how much she liked him. He'd proven again, over the last few days, to be a man of faithfulness, loyalty, and devotion with how much he cared about his dad and his family. His love for them was deep and solid.

He'd been sweet to her too. He'd watched over her and worried about her during the couple of days that they'd been at the hospital. He'd tried to get her to rest, had encouraged her to eat, had brought her more cups of coffee than she could keep count of.

She'd felt his concern and had nearly melted under his tenderness. Yet every time she was with T.W. and saw how rapidly his condition had deteriorated, she knew she had to resist Tyler so that she wasn't distracted from her work again.

She loathed having to avoid him, loathed seeing the disappointment in his eyes when she turned down his offer to play games, when she said she couldn't take a break to eat with him, or when she didn't linger to talk to him.

As much as she didn't want to hurt him, the best thing was to sever their relationship before it had time to grow. She couldn't give in to her desire to be with him. Instead, she needed to pour all her time and energy into T.W., watching over him and taking care of him…the way she should have been watching over him and taking care of him all along.

That was the problem. She'd failed T.W., and she'd never failed a patient before.

She'd been so focused on Tyler those last days before the intestinal obstruction that she hadn't kept a close enough eye on T.W. She should have seen the oncoming pain, should have paid attention to the soreness he'd been experiencing, should have been more aware of his changing condition.

After striving so hard to be the best nurse that Premier had on staff, she'd only proven herself to be the most easily swayed by a handsome man. Of course, there was nothing wrong with her taking a day off. It was true that a person who practiced self-care had an easier time taking care of someone else, and that applied to nurses even more.

But she'd broken her personal rule not to get involved with a client's family. She shouldn't have allowed herself to care about Tyler, and she shouldn't have let T.W. persuade her to go out and spend an entire day with Tyler. They most certainly shouldn't have been together in the hot spring so long.

The stupidest thing of all had been initiating the kiss. In hindsight, she wasn't sure what had come over her or why she'd thought for even a second that kissing Tyler McQuaid was a good idea. Kissing him had been like touching burning hot flames. And she'd felt seared all the way through ever since.

The truth was, if they hadn't been kissing in the hot spring, maybe they would have checked their phones sooner and realized something was wrong. At the very least, after the long day away, they should have gone back to the house, and she should have checked on T.W.

The rational side of her brain told her that even if they'd known what was going on, they wouldn't have been able to do anything at the house, and they would have had to fly T.W. to the emergency room anyway.

Even so, that didn't stop her from berating herself for not catching the problem earlier. Ultimately, she'd proven that Tyler had been right...she wasn't the best nurse for taking care of T.W.

She'd called her agency the first day at the hospital and informed Pippa she needed a replacement right away. Thankfully, Doreen, one of their most competent nurses and an older woman with years of experience, had just finished a position and agreed to travel to Colorado and take care of T.W.

Kinsey only felt a little guilty for making the switch

without consulting T.W. or Tyler. After all, her time there was almost finished anyway. Now, with T.W.'s setback, he would benefit from having the nursing care a while longer, since he wouldn't be strong enough to start chemotherapy for a few more weeks.

The delay was her fault. If the cancer spread even more and caused additional issues, she would blame only herself.

Her heart pinched, and she smoothed a hand over T.W.'s forehead. She'd grown to care about T.W. as she did most of her patients. But this time, the bond with him seemed deeper, and that scared her.

"Hey," came Tyler's soft greeting from the doorway—a greeting that was warm enough to turn her insides into gooey chocolate.

"Hi." She began picking up the bedside table, avoiding looking in his direction, afraid that if she caught even a glimpse of him, she'd melt even more.

His footsteps padded into the room. "I thought you might want this."

The aroma of freshly brewed coffee filled the air. "Thank you, Tyler. You're so thoughtful."

He drew closer until he was standing behind her.

"You can set it on the table." She still didn't let herself look at him and instead focused on organizing T.W.'s bottles of medicine.

Tyler had already been in to check on T.W. earlier,

but because Leah had still been in the room, Kinsey had been able to avoid talking to Tyler directly.

But now...how long could she shuffle around the medicines without being insufferably rude?

He stepped closer, and his hand shot out and covered hers, bringing her fidgeting to a halt.

She stood unmoving, staring at his tanned hand against hers, the sinews and veins so strong, his fingers hard and calloused yet gentle. The muscles in his arm were rigid, and his bicep brushed against her.

His other arm wrapped around her so that he was holding the cup in front of her, a waft of steam filling her senses with the rich aroma of the coffee...and of him.

His warmth, his woodsy scent, his strength encompassed her so that her body was suddenly alert and alive and tuned in to him. He was boxing her in from behind, giving her no place to go, no escape from his presence. She could feel the rise and fall of his chest that was barely touching her back. She could hear the steady rhythm of his breathing. She could almost taste the deliciousness of his nearness.

She couldn't let herself think about his deliciousness. But her rebellious mind went back to their kiss, to the crushing power of his lips, to the stark desire that had been in every move of his mouth.

There was no sense in denying it. She'd loved their kiss. She'd dreamed about their kiss. And she definitely wanted to repeat that kiss, even though she never would.

Releasing a tense breath, she took the coffee, needing for him to step back, needing to put a safe distance between them.

But instead of backing away, he lifted his free hand to her hair and brushed it away from her neck. With her hair still long and loose and not yet pulled back, his fingers skimmed the strands to one side, leaving a stretch of her neck and shoulder visible.

"Dad's finally asleep?" Tyler whispered.

She glanced at T.W. His eyes were closed, his features relaxed, and his breathing even. "Yes," she whispered back.

"Then you can take a few minutes to rest." His fingers skimmed her hair again.

She shouldn't keep standing there with Tyler so near. It wouldn't be fair to either of them to nurture any feelings. Not when she was leaving tomorrow, not when she didn't plan to have a serious relationship with him.

She bent and placed the coffee mug on the bedside table, hoping to break this tentative connection with him. But in the next instant, his fingers moved to the bare spot of her neck and glided the length to her collar bone.

The touch sent electric currents over her skin, zinging down her arm to the tips of her fingers. Those currents weren't ordinary. They were designed to create an immediate and strong need for more of his touch, more of him, more of his affection.

As if realizing the same, his fingers swept around again to her hair and to the back of her neck, where he grazed a line straight down her spine so that his hand ended at the small of her back.

She was half tempted to lean into him, or at the very least to arch her neck and give him more access to it. But she somehow managed to keep her sanity, even though it was slim.

"Please, Kinsey." His whisper came from beside her ear. "I miss you."

She closed her eyes. He'd said the same thing to her at the hospital, and the words went straight to her heart, filling her with a sweet longing she didn't understand.

The truth was, she missed him too. She missed talking with him, missed his dark eyes upon her, missed his smile, missed his presence even when they were just watching a show.

But it didn't matter, did it? She'd already decided she couldn't stay at the ranch. Not when T.W. needed someone else.

Besides, it was ludicrous to think that she and Tyler could have a long-distance relationship. They were both too busy and focused on their careers. She'd never ask him to give up his aspirations just for her, and how could she give up such an important part of herself for him? If she did, what if she eventually resented that decision?

No, she'd already made up her mind that she needed to move on, especially while the feelings between them were so new. It would be easier to rip the Band-Aid off in one swift move than to try to date for a while and realize it wouldn't work and hurt each other even more.

His hand moved from the small of her back to her hip. In the same motion, he bent his head in so that his lips grazed her neck. The touch was so light she almost couldn't feel him. But it was also enough that she had to grasp his hand at her hip to hold herself up.

As her fingers dug into him, his mouth made full contact with her throat.

She gasped, the pleasure of his kiss so exquisite that she could only close her eyes and tilt her head again, wanting more of him.

But she couldn't. She shouldn't. She wouldn't.

His fingers on her hip shifted, splayed, tightened. Then his lips pressed into her neck again more forcefully as he made a trail down to the base of her throat.

When his mouth connected with the tender spot on her shoulder, she gasped again. Oh, heaven. And oh, Tyler. This man was too hard to resist. Why was she even trying so hard to resist him? She didn't know. The truth was, she wanted more of him. So much more.

Maybe if she gave herself just one more moment with him, she'd have her fill. At the very least, she could kiss him again and get the desire out of her system.

She circled around so that she was face-to-face with him and his work-hardened and well-defined body.

He didn't say anything to her, but as his gaze swept across her face, his eyes brimmed with an adoration and a reverence for her that he wasn't trying to hide. In fact, he seemed to be letting her see everything—all the desire, all the feelings, all the need for her that he would no longer hold back.

No one had ever looked at her this way before, as if she were the only thing that mattered in the whole world.

She couldn't stop herself from reaching up both hands, cupping his face, and dragging him down.

His eyes didn't let go of hers. They were solid heat, like a rod of blazing iron, searing into her and branding her as his.

As her lips meshed with his, she sank against him. His mouth met hers eagerly, as if he'd been waiting for days— since their last kiss—for the chance to do this again.

Her lashes fell, and she could only helplessly fall into him, kissing him with all the desire she'd tried to ignore but couldn't.

His lips tangled back with the same intensity as the last time, not at all tentative or timid. He was just as forceful and demanding, and she loved it. She loved the way he kissed, the way it showed how much he adored her. Every stroke of his mouth carried a message that the kiss wasn't just for him but that he cared about her and wanted her because there was nothing else that could compare.

Such kisses laden with so much adoration were addictive. If she'd ever rationalized that kissing him here and now would satisfy her and she'd be able to move on without needing him, she'd been wrong. Instead of being content with his kisses, she was only greedy for more.

She found herself spiraling into an oblivion where only Tyler existed. He was more important to her than anything else.

Her chest welled with such emotion that it hurt. He was her everything, he was her life, he was her future...

Was he really?

A sudden and swift fear snagged onto her chest. It was the same sudden and swift fear she'd had when she'd watched Madison take her last breaths.

The fear pulsed into her throat, choking her, so that she wrenched away from Tyler. The panic was prodding her hard, and she frantically glanced around the room for a place to go, a place that was safe, a place where she could hide from the fear.

With the pounding of dread in every step, she crossed into the bathroom and closed the door behind her. She leaned back and pressed a hand to her chest, as if that could somehow calm the wild beating inside.

What had she just done by kissing Tyler that way? What was she thinking?

20

Tyler tried to calm his uneven breathing, but he was still drowning in Kinsey's kiss without any way to resurface.

The truth was that her kisses were life-altering. With each one, he was dying a little more to himself, and she was becoming more important.

Was that what true love was supposed to be like? A continual sacrifice for the other person?

He braced his head against the outside of the bathroom door, his knees shaking, his heart pounding, and his body thrumming.

Whatever the case, her kisses were powerful enough to undo him. He was like Samson from the Bible when Delilah had cut off his long hair and rendered him completely powerless. If the Philistines had burst into the bedroom at the ranch, they could have tied him up and carried him off and he wouldn't have been able to resist them.

He had to get himself under control so that he could talk to Kinsey and assure her everything would be all right. When she'd pulled back, he'd seen the fear in her eyes, and when she'd run away from him, he'd known it was because she was afraid.

But of what? Had he scared her with the intensity of what he felt for her? After the talk a few weeks ago that he'd had with Dad about getting married, maybe she was worried he was moving too fast.

It was past time for him to have a candid conversation with her about their relationship. In fact, he should have had that conversation before kissing her again.

He released an exasperated sigh—one directed at himself. He was so in love with her that the second she touched him, he lost all rational thought. Every time they kissed, he lost track of reality.

He needed to be careful, go slower, and try to hold back a little bit more.

"Kinsey?" he whispered, throwing a glance over his shoulder toward the bed. His dad hadn't moved, was still sleeping soundly. Thank the good Lord for that. Tyler could only imagine his dad's reaction if he'd awoken to find them kissing so passionately.

Not that his dad would have been upset. No, his dad liked Kinsey a lot and had been playing matchmaker for a while. Most likely, if he'd caught them kissing, he would have called the local preacher over and tried to get them married today.

Tyler dropped his voice even lower. "Can I come in?"

"No." Her answer was hardly more than a whisper in return.

"Please?" He didn't care that he was begging.

She seemed to be hesitating, then a few seconds later, the door clicked open.

He pushed it wider and slipped through.

Kinsey stood against the double sink vanity, her head pressed into her hands.

He left the door open a sliver, partly because it seemed indecent to stand in a bathroom with a woman and also because he didn't want to get so distracted that he couldn't hear Dad in the other room.

"We need to talk, Tyler," she whispered.

"I was just going to say the same thing."

With her shoulders slumped, she was still cradling her head in her hands. Her breathing was faster than usual too.

He hadn't been mistaken that she'd enjoyed their kissing. He'd felt it in the pressure of her mouth, the hunger, the eagerness. He doubted she'd liked it as much as he had. He doubted anyone ever could. But she hadn't hidden her enthusiasm for kissing him. Hadn't she been the one, again, to initiate it? Or maybe he had when he'd kissed her neck.

Either way, they'd both kissed each other passionately. Now he needed to tell her how he really felt about her and about them so that she didn't think he was leading her on or taking advantage of her.

"Kinsey—"

"Tyler, I—"

They both spoke at the same time.

She lifted her head and straightened, as though gathering the strength to say what she needed to. From the fear that still filled her eyes, he had the feeling he wasn't going to like it.

That meant he needed to speak first and fast. But what?

She opened her mouth to talk.

"I love you." His words came out with a fervor he couldn't contain.

Her lips stalled, and her eyes rounded.

"I know it's soon, that we haven't known each other long, but it doesn't matter." He drew in another steadying breath and pushed forward. "You're the one for me—the love of my life that I've been waiting to find."

She watched him for another moment before dropping her chin and staring at the tiled floor.

He waited for a response, his nerves tightening with every passing second. He didn't expect her to declare her love in response, but he wanted some indication she was feeling something similar.

"I'm leaving tomorrow," she blurted.

"What?" The news hit him like a fist in the stomach. "Why?"

"I called Premier and asked them to send a replacement for me."

"I don't understand."

She lifted her gaze, revealing her tortured eyes. "You were right from the beginning. I'm not the best nurse for your dad. He needs someone more dedicated and experienced than me, someone who doesn't abandon him and neglect his care because she's too distracted by his handsome son."

Protest welled up inside Tyler. "No, I was wrong about you. You are the best nurse for him, the only one we want. I know Dad feels the same way."

"I neglected T.W., and now I've set him back." Her face was creased with guilt. "He'll need several more weeks of recuperation before he'll be strong enough again. And if the cancer spreads, it'll be my fault."

Was that the truth? It couldn't be. "You did everything you could—"

"I'm trained to look for signs of regression and pain and problems. If I'd been paying better attention, I would have noticed he was having trouble."

"That's not true…" Even if it was, Tyler could admit he'd had a role in it. He'd been the one to push her to spend time with him, had come in every night to be with her, had caused her to stop being single-minded in her care of Dad.

If anything, he was more to blame than she was with how much time he'd spent distracting her.

"I'm taking myself off the case." Her voice was weary and sad. "Doreen arrives tomorrow. She's older and more experienced and will do a fantastic job."

Should he protest more? Or should he accept a new nurse? After all, this was Dad's life they were talking about. He couldn't jeopardize Dad's life because he was in love with Kinsey and wanted her to stay. If a different nurse would do a better job, then that was the most important thing, wasn't it?

She rubbed a hand across her eyes, wiping away moisture. "I should have listened to you from the start and let someone else handle T.W.'s care. I'm sorry I insisted. I'm sorry I let myself lose my focus. And I'm sorry that now I have to disappoint you."

Disappoint didn't begin to describe the emotions swirling in his chest—confusion and frustration mingled with hurt and panic. He didn't know what to do under the circumstances, but he did know he couldn't lose her. "Just because you want to leave doesn't mean we have to end what we have."

"We don't have anything yet."

He'd just poured out his heart to her, told her he loved her. And this was how she intended to respond? To throw it all back in his face as if it meant nothing to her?

"It would be easier to part ways now, Tyler," she said earnestly, "than to try to have a long-distance relationship."

How could she even think that? "It would be a lot harder for me to give you up than to have a long-distance relationship."

"You know we both want different things out of life. You never wanted a woman like me who isn't from around here. Even if I stayed, I'd constantly be leaving for work. And you didn't want that either. You didn't want to have another woman like Stephanie."

Her words stabbed into him and pierced his heart. Was she right?

How could they make a relationship work if she was gone as a traveling nurse for weeks at a time? Would he eventually feel abandoned, like he had with Stephanie? Would he grow resentful and frustrated again?

He supposed a part of him had hoped Kinsey would be willing to stay and stop all the traveling, that maybe she'd consider taking a nursing job in the area and settling down. But if she had her heart set on being a traveling nurse, how could he ask her to give it up? He couldn't. That wouldn't be fair to her.

Kinsey was watching him, her eyes now filled with determination as if she'd already made up her mind.

"So you're willing to walk away"—the pain inside him stirred into anger—"without trying to find a way to make it work?"

"How can we make it work, Tyler?" Her voice held a thread of anguish.

"You care about me." Maybe she didn't yet love him to the same degree he did her, but she did care. That much was obvious. "Why can't we at least talk about it? Find a compromise?"

"Because I know I'm not what you're looking for and that eventually I'll make you unhappy."

"Your leaving will make me unhappy." Maybe he was being naïve. Maybe she really was too much like Stephanie and he just needed to accept that.

She sighed. "I'm sorry, Tyler. I'm a wandering nomad, and that's probably all I'll ever be."

She'd admitted that she didn't have a home anymore, that she liked the freedom of moving from place to place. But why? Why didn't she want more permanence in her life? Didn't she ever get tired of the short stays and always having to leave people behind? Didn't she want to build deeper relationships? At least with him?

Or what about the fear he'd seen in her eyes? Maybe she was afraid to settle down. Maybe she was afraid because she'd already lost one person she loved— Madison—and she was worried about losing someone important to her again.

The thought rolled through his head, picking up momentum. "You know what I think?" His tone turned hard. "I think you like to move around all the time because then you can keep all your relationships shallow."

She stiffened and backed up against the vanity, the mirror reflecting the stiffness of her back. "My relationships aren't all shallow."

"Yep. You don't let your relationships go too far or get too deep. Since you know you're leaving, you can do your job without getting attached."

"That's not true—"

"You're running away. Then you don't have to worry about losing again like you lost Madison."

She glared at him, her legs suddenly shaking. "How dare you bring her up and use her against me."

At the hurt lacing her voice, the anger inside his chest drained away. "I'm sorry. I shouldn't have."

Kinsey held his gaze a moment longer, the sorrow in her eyes crushing him.

The subject was obviously still too tender for her, the loss too personal. Even four years after the death, it was clear she still had baggage that she hadn't gotten rid of.

With a toss of her hair, she moved past him, opened the door, and started back toward his dad.

He didn't move, could only stare at the empty spot where she'd just been standing. It reflected the emptiness in his heart.

If it was that easy for her to walk away from him, then perhaps he'd been wrong about his love. What if he was only infatuated with her and had gotten carried away with his feelings? What if he'd let the bargain with his dad influence him too much so that he'd put aside sound reasoning when it came to picking a spouse? What if he'd allowed his emotions to eradicate rational thoughts?

He might be confused and clueless about a lot, but there was one thing he did know. She was giving up on them before they'd had the chance to get started. And maybe it was for the best to let her go now while he still could.

21

"Darlin'," T.W. said earnestly, "I don't want any other nurse but you."

Kinsey patted T.W.'s hand. This goodbye was much harder than she'd expected, more difficult than usual because normally she was not as attached to her patients as she was to T.W. Normally she didn't blur the personal and professional lines the same way she had with this case. And normally she was able to care about her patients without creating lasting bonds.

But T.W. and the McQuaids were different.

"Doreen's a wonderful lady," she reassured T.W. "She'll take good care of you. I promise."

T.W.'s face was haggard as he lay against the mound of plumped pillows in his elevated hospital bed. "I don't understand why I need someone else."

Kinsey had already explained herself to T.W. and Leah yesterday, not long after she'd told Tyler. Even though the conversation with T.W. had been tough, it hadn't been as hard as the one with Tyler. That had been so painful she'd hardly been able to think or breathe afterward.

The rest of yesterday had been extremely difficult, and Tyler had avoided her most of the day and night. She'd only seen him in passing, and even those encounters had been brief and tense. It had been easy to see she'd hurt him with her rejection after he'd told her he loved her.

He'd told her that he loved her.

The awe of it spread through her again as it had every time she'd thought about it. He hadn't spoken the words casually or lightly. No, he'd said them as if he'd deeply meant them, as if he truly believed she was the love of his life and the one he wanted to be with forever.

How was it possible that he already knew? He couldn't feel that strongly about her. Not yet.

T.W. clasped her hand and peered up at her intently. "Tyler really loves you, Kinsey."

She startled at T.W.'s declaration, almost as if he'd been able to see the conflict battling inside her head. Or maybe he'd seen the conflict waging war in her expression.

"You'll eventually feel the same way about him," T.W. continued. "You won't have a choice, really. Not when he decides he wants to make you his. He'll win you over, and you'll be helpless to resist."

"T.W.," she gently chided, lifting a hand to his cheek. All the affection for this dear man rose swiftly and brought tears to the backs of her eyes. "Tyler and I...we're going our separate ways. We already decided that." She'd been the one to decide and hadn't really given Tyler any other option.

Of course, he could have tried protesting a little more. Followed her out of the bathroom, maybe even approached her later in the day to talk about it again. But he hadn't. He'd been quiet, almost sullen—the same way he'd been when she'd first arrived—and had hardly spoken to her.

Not that she wanted him to protest or follow her or approach her again. It was for the best that he'd respected her decision and let her go, wasn't it? She'd been right that things couldn't work out between them. Not when he needed a woman who wanted the permanence that the ranch represented.

That wasn't her.

"You can make this easy or hard." T.W. gave her a weak smile. "I'd suggest you make it easy and just admit you belong with Tyler."

"We're too different."

T.W. shook his head. "Naw. You're perfect for each other. I saw it from the first day."

"That's just because you're a hopeless romantic." She smiled at him. She would miss him dearly.

He searched her face. "So you're gonna make this hard on him, are you?"

"T.W., please." She glanced toward her suitcases, already packed and ready to go. "I have to go. And I want to say goodbye and tell you I'll be praying for you and keeping tabs on you."

"That's fine, darlin'. You go ahead and make it hard on him. All the McQuaid men have had to fight to keep their women. It makes the lovin' all the sweeter."

Kinsey bent and pressed a kiss to T.W.'s forehead. "I'll miss you."

As she straightened and began to step back, he grabbed her hand. "You've become like a daughter to me, Kinsey. And I'll look forward to the day when Tyler brings you back, because he will. Mark my word."

She needed to contradict T.W. and set him straight. Again. But she'd learned how much he wanted to see all his children married. He longed for them to be settled and happy the way he was with Leah, so she couldn't be upset at him for pushing her and Tyler together.

She gave T.W. a final hug before rolling her suitcases out of his room. Tyler was waiting in the kitchen with Leah and Emberly. She hugged both women and then faced Tyler, who was leaning against the counter, every inch of him rugged cowboy.

A part of her wanted to hug him goodbye too. But before she could step up to him, he grabbed hold of both of her suitcases and began to carry them out of the house. Silently and stiffly, he walked ahead of her up the stairway that led to the helicopter landing pad.

Kade was already there ready to take her to the airport. While in Denver, he would also pick up Doreen, whose flight would be landing soon. Kade stowed Kinsey's luggage away, then hopped inside and told her to take all the time she needed, insinuating that she and Tyler would want a lengthy goodbye.

But she didn't need to say much since she'd already said everything yesterday. He helped her up into the helicopter, his dark eyes somber, his expression severe. The light that had been there was gone.

Her heart weighed heavily in her chest as she sat back in her seat. Was she making a mistake by not giving them a chance? Was she running away as he'd accused?

She held his gaze for several more seconds. If he asked her to stay one last time, would she? Would he dare? And would she dare in return?

He lifted a hand toward her face, as though he intended to caress her cheek.

She held her breath, suddenly aching for him and his touch, uncertain how she'd survive another minute, much less a lifetime, without it.

But in the next instant, he dropped his hand and took a step back. "Take care, Kinsey."

She nodded, unable to get her voice working, afraid if

she spoke, it would tremble.

He closed the door. Then with his usual long stride, he walked toward the stairs and began to descend...all without a single look back.

A moment later, when the helicopter rose, she couldn't keep from peering out the window, hoping for a glimpse of him. The ranch sprawled out for acres—the guest homes, the barn and corral, the lodge with the magnificent dining room, the ropes course, and even the hot springs with the elegant pools and bathhouse.

Her time there had been too busy to experience all the luxuries and adventures the ranch offered, but she'd gotten to take part in much more than she'd ever thought she would. The McQuaids had welcomed her in like she was one of their family and had made her feel at home.

Home.

Even though she still had her bedroom at her childhood house where her mom lived, she didn't belong there anymore. She hadn't since Madison had died and her parents had split. Was that because a house wasn't really a home without the love of a family to make it that way? Was that why the McQuaids' ranch had such a homey feel to it? Because they loved one another so deeply?

Her thoughts swirled in rhythm with the chopper blades. Was she missing out on love because she kept her relationships shallow? Tyler had accused her of doing so, of moving on so that she didn't get attached. He'd even brought up losing Madison as if that explained everything.

Kinsey pressed her fingers to her temples to ease the ache from the tiredness and sorrow of leaving someone else. Had she kept herself from getting close to people because of how much it had hurt to lose Madison?

Of course, she'd always known she wanted to be a nurse, ever since Madison's first time struggling through RSV. Kinsey'd had her toy stethoscope and toy blood pressure cuff and had pretended to help her sister during the entire time she'd struggled to get better.

But she'd never planned to be a traveling nurse. Not until after Madison had died. The desire to do so might have been altruistic, might have been inspired by seeing how much Pippa liked being a traveling nurse. Yet, at the time, Kinsey had been ready to get away from the painful memories and to escape from the bitterness of her parents' divorce.

Had she been running away from the pain ever since?

Maybe Tyler was right. Maybe that was why she kept on accepting new traveling nurse positions—because then she never got too attached to anyone. She could leave before the bonds became too close…like they'd become with the McQuaids.

If only she'd made plans to go when she'd first started falling in love with Tyler…

The whirring in her head came to an abrupt halt.

First started falling in love? She hadn't fallen in love with Tyler, had she?

Her mind replayed all the moments she'd had with him since she'd arrived at Healing Springs Ranch—the good ones as well as the challenging ones. With every memory that rolled through her head, her heart ached even more.

By the time the helicopter touched down at the airport, her heart felt as though it had been ripped into shreds and scattered over the bottom of her chest.

As the blades and engine silenced, Kade didn't move from his seat. Instead, he sat quietly, drumming his fingers on his thigh.

She couldn't make herself move either, almost as if she were paralyzed.

Kade finally shifted in his pilot's seat so that he was looking at her. "You're making a mistake in leaving him."

She didn't have to ask who *him* was to know Kade was referring to Tyler.

Kade's dark-brown eyes, so much like Tyler's, were filled with determination. "You know about the McQuaid legacy of love, don't you?"

"No."

"It's said of the McQuaid men that when they fall in love, there's no going back. It's fast, furious, and forever."

"Did Tyler tell you that he loves me?" Did his whole

family know?

Kade's lips quirked up on one side in a sad grin. "Tyler didn't have to say a single word for all of us to see that he fell fast and furious and forever."

Fast. Furious. Forever. Was that kind of love possible? Especially when the hardships of life crowded in?

Forever hadn't been part of her parents' marriage. Their marriage had probably already been weak when Madison's leukemia came along and caused an even bigger rift. Dad had pushed for more experimental drugs and had wanted to enroll Madison in additional research programs. But Mom had doted on Madison and had always chosen to do whatever Madison wanted, whether it had been sound reasoning or not.

Kinsey had tried to stay in the middle, not taking either side, trying to help Madison stay alive but also respecting her sister's wishes not to drag out the end of her life and the pain and misery.

"What's holding you back, Kinsey?" Kade asked.

What was holding her back from embracing the love Tyler was offering her? It wasn't really the traveling or her freedom or even her wanting to experience more of the country. She'd already seen more than enough and experienced more places and people than most.

Was it fear? Fear of letting herself love again when she could lose that person?

She sighed heavily. "Honestly?"

He nodded, clearly waiting for her answer.

"I'm a wimp." She'd witnessed so much bravery from her patients in facing their difficulties. Maybe it was time to take a lesson from them and face her problems instead of running from them.

Kade's eyes brightened. "You know what they say about being a wimp, don't you?"

"I don't know, Kade. I don't know if I can be brave."

"They say the best way to gain courage is to climb your mountain."

She wasn't sure she was ready to climb her mountain, to make a change, to push through the fears. After walking away from her fears for so long, the easy and level path beckoned to her.

At the ping of an incoming text, Kade read the message and then began to type a response.

She started to reach behind her for one of her suitcases. She had a few hours before her flight left. Even so, she didn't need to bother Kade any longer.

He glanced up from his phone and then waved at someone exiting from the nearby terminal gate. The morning sunshine poured over a robust woman with short, curly black hair and an extra pep to her step.

Kinsey sat forward. "Pippa?"

The dear woman waved as she crossed to the helicopter.

"What's Pippa doing here?"

Kade was already opening his door and stepping out. He bounded over to Pippa and shook her hand. All the while, Kinsey could only stare at her friend.

As Pippa and Kade began to walk back to the helicopter, Kinsey finally unbuckled and climbed out. When her feet touched the ground, Pippa was there, wrapping her up in her big arms. "Girl, it's good to see you."

Kinsey hugged her friend back, surprised at how much relief she felt at seeing the woman.

Pippa pulled back and held Kinsey out at arm's length, perusing her from her head to her toes. "Just like I thought. You're more beautiful than ever and causing all kinds of trouble up here because of it."

Kinsey laughed. "That's not true."

"Oh, it's true all right. My phone's been ringing practically nonstop since you told T.W. you were leaving yesterday."

Kinsey's smile fell away. "He's been calling?"

"Oh yeah, and he's had his kids calling too." She nodded at Kade, who was now loading her suitcase into the back of the helicopter.

"I already explained everything to everyone, that T.W. deserves a more competent nurse."

"Yes, ma'am, but they told me they want you to stay on the case, that it would be more detrimental to T.W.'s health if you left him at this point."

"That's not true. He's doing great, and he'll do even better with someone who isn't distracted."

Pippa reached up and patted her cheek. "Listen, girl. I've already heard the story of T.W.'s obstruction about a dozen times now, so it doesn't matter what you say. I know for a fact you're being too hard on yourself."

"I'm not—"

"Girl, don't deny it. I know you well enough." A plane taking off roared above them.

Kinsey hesitated. Had she been too hard on herself? It was possible. The obstruction could have developed without any warning. Or it could have happened quickly. T.W. had assured her she hadn't done anything wrong or missed any symptoms. So why was she blaming herself? "Maybe I am being a little too hard on myself."

"Good, then you'll go back and finish the job." Pippa started toward the door of the helicopter.

"What?"

"You heard me. You're not quitting on one of our best customers, especially when they offered to pay double your rate to have you stay and are giving a sizable donation to our agency once the job is complete."

Kinsey could only stare after her friend as she tried to make sense of what the McQuaids were doing. They weren't letting her quit. At the very least, they were making it difficult, especially for Premier, who stood to benefit if they made her cooperate.

"This is bribery," Kinsey called out.

Kade just grinned as he fidgeted with something on the side of the helicopter.

"You knew about this?" she asked him.

He tipped up his hat to reveal his merry eyes. "Yep."

"Does Tyler?"

"Nope. Not yet."

"So Doreen isn't coming?"

Pippa paused in climbing up into the helicopter. "I'll be filling in for you during the next three days to give you a break. But then you're finishing up instead of running off with your tail tucked between your legs."

Kinsey folded her arms across her chest and glared at her friend. "Don't I have a choice in the matter?"

"No, ma'am."

She nodded at the airport terminal. "What about my flight?"

"It's cancelled." With that, Pippa plopped down into one of the back seats.

Kinsey wanted to be mad, but Pippa was right, as usual.

Slowly, Kinsey stepped up into the helicopter. She needed to finish the job she'd started. It was unprofessional for her not to, especially because she had the most insight into T.W.'s issues, and he would benefit from the consistency.

Yes, she'd go back, and she would get to see Tyler

again.

Could she be brave enough to face him? And if she faced him, then what? The very real truth was that he might not want her. Not after she'd rejected him.

During the helicopter ride back to the ranch, Kinsey wanted to talk more with Pippa about the circumstances—whom exactly she'd talked to, and whether Tyler had been involved in the plan. But the noise prevented anything beyond a few shouted words.

When Kade finally began to descend, Kinsey's pulse picked up speed. What would Tyler say when he saw she was back?

She glanced out the window to find unfamiliar terrain and a different landing pad.

Kade brought the helicopter to a halt and cut the engine, then hopped out at the approach of a young man and woman, both beaming. He gave them each a hug, then began chatting with them.

Maybe this was just a detour on the way back to the ranch. If so, it was a very pretty detour. They were in a narrow mountain valley with majestic cliffs rising all around. The granite was jagged and imposing, with thick pine trees growing out of the stone—or so it seemed. On one side of the grassy area where they'd landed, a lovely log cabin was nestled against a valley wall. On the other side, a dozen smaller rustic cabins overlooked a river that sparkled in the morning sunshine.

The place looked like a restful haven, a getaway from the busyness of life.

Pippa had risen from her seat and was dragging one of Kinsey's suitcases from the back. "Have a nice three days, girl."

Kinsey sat up straight and blinked. "You want me to stay here?"

Pippa shrugged. "Kade suggested it, said he knows the owners and that they had a cabin open for you."

Kade was now jogging back toward the helicopter. The young couple stood arm in arm, watching him and peering at her too.

A part of Kinsey was intrigued and wanted to embrace staying in this remote getaway for a few days. It would probably do her good. She needed some time away to rest and take a break from the demands of being a traveling nurse. And maybe while she was here, she could also sort out her feelings for Tyler.

Kade opened the door and extended a hand to her. "It's all set."

"What is?"

"Your mini vacation."

She took his hand and allowed him to help her out, this time noting the horses grazing in a pasture of wildflowers on one side of the main cabin, and a large garden on the other surrounded by a tall wire fence. A log cabin barn stood a short distance away with a cow grazing in a penned-in area.

"Camp Ponderosa is one of the prettiest and most secluded camps in the Rockies." Kade was peering over the landscape too. "Mitch and Anna managed to free up one of the cabins for three days."

"It is pretty." She drew in a deep breath.

His attention returned to her, and his expression turned solemn. "I know we did all this behind your back. But I hope you know it's because we care about you and Tyler."

A lump pushed up into her throat. "I know."

"Good."

"It'll give me some time to think." She needed it. She could no longer shove aside her poor way of coping with all that had happened in her family. She finally had to face it with courage. "Maybe I'll climb my mountain here."

His brows lifted above questioning eyes, then as understanding dawned at his reference from earlier, he smiled. "Oh yeah, you'll definitely get your chance to do that here."

She hoped so. Because when she next faced Tyler, she wanted to have the courage to run to him instead of away.

22

Tyler slammed the stall door shut, then tossed the shovel against the wall, where it fell to the ground with a loud *clank*.

He was going crazy without Kinsey.

She'd only been gone for eight hours, and it already felt like eight years.

He paced the length of the open center aisle, his boots thumping the cement floor in pace with his heart, which was demanding that he go after her.

He paused and looked at his watch again, as he had for the hundredth time over the past hours. Her flight would have left by now for O'Hare. In fact, she was probably already landing in Chicago, maybe even on her way to her mom's house, where she stayed between jobs.

Kade had arrived at the ranch with the new nurse hours ago. But it hadn't been Doreen. Instead, it was Kinsey's friend Pippa, the one she'd talked about from time to time who had been there to help with her sister's care.

Pippa had been good so far. But she was much louder and brasher than Kinsey. And bossier. She'd shooed him out of his dad's room twice already in the past few hours. Kinsey had never done that, had always welcomed—and even encouraged—the family's visits.

Tyler suspected it wouldn't have mattered if Florence Nightingale had come back from the grave and offered to be the new nurse. He probably would have found something wrong with her or something he didn't like. Because she wasn't Kinsey.

He paused at the outer barn door and peered over the corral and the new mares along with the other horses that were grazing on the slender shoots of buffalograss. The afternoon was still sunny, but the clouds forming on the western range meant that a storm was brewing. The weather app confirmed they were in for evening thundershowers.

The truth was, if he planned to go after Kinsey, then he needed to do it soon, or he'd be stuck until tomorrow—at least, if he wanted Kade to fly him to Denver.

But the dilemma was whether he should go after her or whether he should give her the freedom that she wanted.

"Shoot." He palmed the back of his neck, the tension

in his muscles almost more than he could bear.

All he wanted to do was be with her. It was the only thing he could think of, the only thing he'd been able to focus on all day, the only thing he wanted with his whole life. He just wanted her. That was it. Plain and simple.

Of course he loved Wyatt and was looking forward to the boy's return at the end of the week. They'd been in touch every day, sometimes even multiple times, and Tyler knew Wyatt was having fun in New York City and that Anson was taking good care of him. Apparently Stephanie was spending time with Wyatt too, now that she was in between husbands. Maybe it helped that Wyatt was older, was more independent, and enjoyed doing more things.

Whatever the case, Tyler loved the kid. But the truth was, Wyatt was growing up, getting busier, and would eventually want to hang out with friends more than with his dad. It was just the natural way of things.

Tyler couldn't hang on to his son forever. Parents were meant to eventually let their children go. But a woman he loved? He was meant to hang on to her forever.

So why hadn't he hung on to Kinsey?

At Kade's voice and laughter from the other end of the barn, Tyler swiveled and retraced his steps down the center aisle between horse stalls to the discarded shovel. As Kade entered through the opposite wide doorway with a coil of rope around his shoulder and a foal trailing behind him, Tyler fidgeted with the shovel, hoping he looked busy.

"Still going crazy, I see," Kade called with a smirk.

"None of your business." Tyler twisted the shovel and then opened the closest stall.

"Don't know what you're waiting for." Kade sauntered down the center aisle.

"I'm waiting for you to zip it up and take a hike."

Kade halted several feet away and leaned against a beam, crossing both his arms and legs. "Don't reckon that's the way you want to be talking to the only one who knows where Kinsey went."

"Thought she went back to Naperville."

"Nope."

Tyler stepped out of the stall, his pulse halting along with every other function in his body. "Where is she?"

Kade shrugged too casually. "She's safe enough. No need to worry."

Tyler released the tension from his shoulders. "Why didn't she go home?"

"Maybe she didn't have much of a choice," Kade said sheepishly.

The tension came rushing back in full force. "What did you do?"

"Whoa now." Kade took a rapid step back. "It wasn't just me. Dad, Mom, and Emberly were all in on the plans too."

"What plans?"

"The plans for you to win her back."

Tyler released a scoffing laugh, even though his heart was racing with charged need. "You had no right to interfere."

"That's a bunch of horse manure, and you know it."

Tyler jabbed the shovel into the hay, closed the stall door, and then turned his full wrathful glare upon his brother. "I don't need anyone else butting into my business with Kinsey. I can handle things on my own."

"And how's that going for you?"

"I've got it under control."

"Is that right? Let's see." Kade lifted his hand and started ticking off his fingers. "She left. You let her go. She's not here. And now you're not doing a blasted thing about it except acting like a baby."

Tyler wanted to growl out his frustration at Kade, but a sliver of rationality stopped him. He wasn't really mad at Kade. He was mad at himself for making such a mess of things.

"So what am I supposed to do?" he practically shouted. "She doesn't want me. She left me. Just like Stephanie did."

"Hold on!" Kade held up a hand. "Kinsey and Stephanie are like day and night. Kinsey actually cares about people, and Stephanie only cares about herself."

At the time of the split-up, Kade had only been in high school and had been busy with his own life and developing his bull-riding skills. Tyler hadn't realized Kade had even paid attention to Stephanie. But apparently he had, because he'd summed up the two women's differences pretty well.

"If you're comparing the situation to Stephanie, then at least do me a favor and compare it the right way." Kade's voice was filled with exasperation. "Kinsey fits in here. She loves Mom and Dad. She likes Colorado. She's energetic and willing to try new things and works hard. Stephanie didn't have any of that."

Kade was right. Stephanie had moved to the ranch expecting to change things to her preference. Not that he'd been opposed to her making changes. But she hadn't made a concerted effort to like his family or learn to like his life. Instead, she'd privately complained to him about everything.

"Even more than that," Kade continued, "Kinsey fits with you. Everyone could see that right away."

"She fits with me perfectly." The ache in Tyler's heart pulsed hard at the thought of how well Kinsey meshed with him—in personality, temperament, activities they enjoyed, energy level, passion, and so many other things.

The fact was, he connected with her on a soul level unlike with any other person. And then there was the chemistry between them that was totally sizzling so that they could hardly be within a few feet of each other without heat sparking to life.

Yes, they had differences too, and they would both have adjustments to make. But he wasn't the same immature man that he'd been with Stephanie. He'd learned from his mistakes and was more sensitive and considerate.

"I know I'll sound like Dad here," Kade said seriously, "but the wisdom bears repeating."

Tyler gave his youngest brother his full attention, surprised that of all his siblings, he was having this conversation with Kade, who knew the least about love and relationships. Or at least Tyler thought he did. Maybe the kid had experienced more love and loss than he let on.

"Dad always said that as men, we need to work really hard to win over that one special woman we're spending forever with. And he always said that the best women are the hardest to win, but the hardest-fought battles bring the sweetest victory."

Tyler could hear his dad saying those very words, had heard his dad say them plenty of times in his life.

So why wasn't he listening? Why wasn't he fighting harder to win the best woman he'd ever met? And blast it all. Why was he standing around the barn doing piddly chores and banging shovels when he could be chasing after Kinsey and trying to win her back?

With a huff, he started stalking down the aisle toward the front of the barn, a sudden urgency lighting a fire under his feet.

"You gonna say anything?" Kade called after him. "Or you planning to ignore me?"

"Not doing either."

"Then what are you doing?"

"Going to get my woman back."

Kade chuckled. "Attaboy."

Tyler made it two feet out the barn door before grinding to a halt in the increasingly cloudy afternoon. He pivoted and looked back to find Kade still leaning casually against the center beam, the foal behind him munching on a stray pile of hay.

Tyler motioned at him. "Well, come on."

"Come on, what?" Kade was grinning like a little girl.

"I need you to take me to her."

"Say please."

Tyler sighed. Kade sure did enjoy annoying him. "Just get your stuff and let's get going before the storm hits."

Kade shook his head. "The storm's already too close."

"Tell me where she is. I'll drive. I want to go now."

"I'm not telling you where she's at." Kade's grin only spread. "You need to give Kinsey a chance to miss you."

Tyler's rampaging thoughts came to a halt. Was Kade right?

"Trust me," Kade said. "I dropped her off, and she

needs the time."

"How much time?"

"Three days."

Tyler didn't want to give her another second. He needed to go right away, draw her into his arms, and kiss her all night if that's what it took to convince her they were right for each other.

He paced several steps forward then back. He took off his hat and jammed his fingers into his hair. Where was the balance between giving her the chance to think about things and letting her know how much he cared about her?

He planned to fight hard to have her—harder than he'd fought for anything else in his life. The problem was, he'd already pushed her away once. How in the world could he keep from pushing her away again?

23

Kinsey considered herself a fit person, but she'd never done anything as hard as climb a fourteener. Her legs ached, her breathing was choppy, and her head pounded.

Had she made a mistake in attempting to scale one of Colorado's highest peaks?

Ahead, Mitch led their small group of hikers. She wanted to call out to him to stop, to give them another break so she could tell him she was quitting and going back.

She paused and grabbed on to the rocky ledge beside her.

The person behind her halted too.

Kinsey gasped for breath and flexed a cramping leg. What had she been thinking?

On the switchback above her, Mitch glanced down, then paused. "Hold up, everyone."

Thankfully, the camp director was a patient man and

hadn't gotten upset at any of them during the past few hours ascending Mount Elbert. He'd been amazing, actually. So had his wife Anna, although she hadn't joined them on the hike.

Kinsey wiped her arm across the perspiration on her forehead. She should have stayed back like Anna. She could have lounged around her cabin like she'd done yesterday after arriving. The ten-by-ten-foot room was very different from the luxurious cabins at Healing Springs Ranch. With a single bunk bed, kitchenette, and tiny bathroom, the cabin was rustic and simple with a small porch that overlooked the river.

Kade had made arrangements with Mitch and Anna to stock her cabin with food and other essentials, so she was comfortable and well taken care of. The two had also assured her she could participate in as few or as many of the guided activities the camp offered as she liked.

She'd considered just sitting in one of the wooden rockers on the porch for the whole visit, reading or taking in the view. But last night, as she'd been rocking and watching several deer grazing along the riverbank, her heart had ached with a longing for Tyler that she hadn't been able to dampen. She'd been gone from him less than twelve hours and already it felt like an eternity.

Her night had been full of dreams of him, the keen longing for him only growing. Missing him had brought back the memories of missing Madison, so that the tightness of fear around her chest had grown too.

By morning, she'd been restless and ready to do something to distract herself. So she'd decided that if she could climb a real mountain, maybe she could climb the metaphorical mountain Kade had mentioned.

She'd been wrong. She couldn't do either.

"How we doing?" Mitch called down to her. Outfitted in the best hiking gear, he was a pro compared to the rest of them, especially her in a baseball cap, running shoes, leggings, and the gopher-face T-shirt.

She waved up at him. "I'll wait right here while you guys finish."

"You sure?" His breathing was as even and calm as if he'd been out taking a leisurely stroll.

She tried for a smile. "I'm tuckered out." That was an understatement.

Mitch studied her as if seeing right through all her excuses. "The end is just ahead, less than thirty minutes."

She shielded the brim of her hat against the late-morning sunshine and attempted to view the trail ahead. It was an endless and steep mountainside full of big rocks, with no view of the top in sight. From her perspective, the climb went on forever.

Mitch followed her gaze. "I know you can't see the pinnacle yet, but it really is coming."

"I believe you. I just don't have the energy to go any farther." Or the desire. She just wanted to go back down.

Mitch pinned her with an intense look. "You have to decide whether you'll hurt yourself more by pushing forward or by holding back."

The statement was profound, and it resonated deep within. What he was saying didn't just apply to the hike but also to everything in life. The truth was that some difficult things might need to be abandoned because of the harm they caused. But other difficult things needed to be endured because giving up would only make a person weak.

Which was it for her?

She didn't have to think long to know that if she gave up now on the hike, and in this difficulty with Tyler, she'd be letting her cowardliness win. But if she challenged herself to persevere, she'd grow stronger—at least, she hoped so.

She dragged a breath into her oxygen-starved lungs, then she gave a nod. "I'll push forward." She had to do it for herself, for Madison, and for the life that could be hers if she made herself keep walking forward instead of holding back.

Mitch gave her an encouraging nod and resumed his steady trek. The others fell into step again, and she moved one foot forward, then the next. She didn't look up but kept her head down, focused on making each tiny climb up even though her legs felt weighed down with hundred-pound ankle bands.

"Almost there!" came a call.

She didn't know who it was, didn't care. She couldn't think of anything but just taking the next step forward.

Finally, as she rounded a bend, the climb ended. A rocky but level area spread out around her. She bent over at the knees and dragged in several breaths. The other hikers from their group milled around her.

Had she really made it?

Mitch stopped beside her. "How you doing?"

"I've been better," she managed.

"Give it a minute, and then you'll be glad you forced yourself to finish."

She felt like she was dying, but she nodded anyway.

The first thing she became conscious of was the wind and the power of the gusts as they blew against her. The second thing was the crispness of the air cooling her skin. Then she noticed the vastness of the sky that surrounded her, so close she could touch it.

When she finally straightened, she felt a moment of dizziness as she took in the view. The entire world seemed to spread out before her, rolling on forever—forests, hills, distant mountain peaks—in every direction she looked.

She took in another breath, and an incredible sense of satisfaction settled over her. She feasted on the beauty, letting it fill her soul with awe. This was what she would have missed if she hadn't forced herself to finish those last grueling steps of the climb. This.

The other hikers were resting, some sitting on rocks, others walking around, a few taking pictures. No one was in a hurry to leave. She certainly wasn't.

She found a secluded spot on a large flat stone. She sprawled out and popped open her water bottle and sipped while she quietly took in the beauty unlike anything she'd ever seen before.

She'd climbed her mountain. If she could do this, she could do anything...including overcoming her fear of getting too close to others. She could return to Healing Springs Ranch, continue to work with T.W., and allow herself to move deeper with people.

More importantly, she could give a relationship with Tyler a chance to develop, couldn't she? She had to stop holding him at arm's length and let him into her heart and life...if she wasn't too late.

At the very least, when she returned to Healing Springs Ranch, she needed to track him down and apologize. She didn't know exactly what she would say or what her apology would entail. She only knew that it was her turn to tell him she was sorry after the many times he'd already done so.

He was a proud and commanding man, and she loved when he was slightly arrogant and bossy with that little quirk of his lips and the flash in his eyes. But she also loved his humility, that he was quick to apologize and make amends.

What had Kade said about the McQuaid legacy of love? That the men in the McQuaid family always loved fast, furiously, and forever. Was that the kind of love Tyler had for her? Maybe that was the kind of love that would make a solid foundation, one that wouldn't crumble when hardships caused disagreements.

Was it possible she could have that kind of love too?

Maybe loving that way was a choice. Just like she'd chosen to climb this fourteener, she had to push herself to keep going, pursue Tyler, and prove to him that she was done running away. Because if she didn't, she would miss out on a mountaintop experience in a relationship with him—a whole world of breathtaking beauty and wonder and delight.

A sense of urgency prodded her to her feet. She wanted to be with Tyler. Not only did she need to apologize, but she also needed to tell him she loved him. Absolutely nothing else was more important than that.

The moment she was back at the campground, she would call Pippa and get Kade's number and ask him to come get her today…if he was willing. She didn't want to impose on him any more than she already had. But she didn't need—or want—to stay at the campground a single second longer. All she wanted was to see Tyler.

She climbed down from the stone and then halted, a sudden burst of fear pulsing through her. What if Tyler had changed his mind about loving her? What if he was angry? What if he'd decided she was too much like his ex-wife after all and didn't want to take the risk that she'd leave and hurt him the same way? Because she had already left and hurt him...

Kinsey pressed a hand against her racing heart. Maybe it would be better to stay at the camp and take the full three days, and then she wouldn't look so desperate. She could return to her nursing job and gauge Tyler's reaction to her. If he were aloof and angry, then she wasn't sure what she'd do.

"No," she whispered with a shake of her head. She had to push past all the fear and uncertainty of the future, especially the fear that she'd lose him.

That meant she had to go and talk to him today.

24

Tyler was being drastic in chasing after Kinsey, but he didn't care. He'd been going literally out-of-his-mind crazy since she'd left the ranch yesterday.

He'd taken Kade's advice and waited through the evening and night, even though he hadn't been able to do anything, not even sleep. When dawn had broken, he'd gone to Kade's apartment above the barn and woken him, begging him to take him to Kinsey. Once again, his brother had encouraged him to wait the three days.

Tyler had tried to wait. He'd gone to his office at the lodge, hoping work would distract him. But he hadn't been able to focus. One thought had pulsed through him over and over—that he had to fight for her and let her know he wasn't willing to give up on her or on them.

With the need to see her only growing more painful, he'd finally convinced Kade to take him to Kinsey. He'd promised Kade he'd say what he needed to, and if Kinsey wasn't ready, he'd walk away and wouldn't pressure her anymore…at least for today.

Kade had nodded and fired up the helicopter. Then they'd taken off.

It hadn't taken Tyler long to figure out where they were going—to Camp Ponderosa near Mount Elbert. Mitch was a distant cousin and a good family friend who'd lived with them for a while. After all the McQuaids had done for him, it was no wonder Kade had turned to Mitch for a return favor in giving Kinsey a place to stay for a few days.

Tyler would have chosen a more comfortable and upscale resort for Kinsey, but at least it was safe and secure, and Mitch and Anna were trustworthy. Tyler supposed he compared everything with his luxury ranch. But he wanted to give Kinsey only the best of everything, including the best of himself.

A short while ago, when they'd landed in a field near the camp, Anna had come out of the barn to greet them, letting them know Kinsey had gone on the hike up Mount Elbert, that the group had at least an hour's head start.

Kade had flown the helicopter to a clearing in one of the higher parts of the trail where Tyler might have been able to catch up with the hikers. But when they'd reached the clearing, Tyler hadn't been able to see anyone and had decided to climb the rest of the distance on his own.

Now, as he made his way up the last of the switchbacks, his lungs and muscles burned. Had he been too pushy to come after her? Had he overstepped? Should he have waited back at the camp like any sane person would have?

Maybe he shouldn't have chased her down at all. What would she say when she saw him coming after her like the lovesick man that he was?

As he ascended the last part of the trail and stepped up onto the top of the mountain, his pulse began to pound hard and his mouth went dry. His gaze swept over the barren, rocky plateau, and he frantically searched for her among the dozen or so hikers that loitered on the peak among the large stones.

Where was she?

He needed to see her—needed her almost more than air.

In the next instant, his gaze snagged on her talking to Mitch a short distance away. Even flushed and wind-tossed after the half-day hike, she was a knockout, especially in the leggings that made her legs look endlessly long and her body perfectly curved. She was wearing a cap with her hair pulled back in a ponytail. And she had on the gopher shirt they'd bought on their day-long nondate.

She could have picked any shirt, but she'd chosen that one. That had to mean something, didn't it? He'd take hope in anything at this point.

Mitch's attention shifted to him.

Immediately, Kinsey's gaze swung his way, giving him a perfect view of her face in all its exquisiteness. She stopped talking mid-sentence, and her bright eyes rounded in disbelief.

Tyler hesitated. Shoot. What was he doing here acting like a stalker? No doubt he'd only send Kinsey running farther from him. Maybe he should have listened to Kade after all. Why hadn't he?

Because he was in love, that's why. Because he was desperately and deeply in love with her, and he wanted her to know that. Even if all he could do today was walk over and tell her, that would be enough. At least for today. He might come back tomorrow and talk to her again. He'd probably come back every day until her time at the camp was done.

If that made him the world's biggest fool, then so be it. He was fighting for her with everything he had and wasn't holding anything back.

Without waiting for an invitation, he started toward her. Even though the ground was uneven and rocky, he was used to such terrain and managed to cover the distance quickly before she could move.

Not that she had any place to go. She was watching his approach with unreadable eyes. She'd finally closed her mouth and wasn't smiling. But she also wasn't glowering at him. So that was good.

He was crossing his fingers she wasn't mad that he'd barged in on her vacation, especially on her hike. Even if she was upset, at least she'd know the lengths he was willing to go to for her and for their relationship.

He stopped when he was a couple feet away.

"Hey, man," Mitch said, glancing back and forth between them.

"Mitch, I need a few minutes with Kinsey." Tyler didn't waste any time on a greeting. He was suddenly too nervous and needed to say what he'd come for before anything interfered.

Mitch started to speak again, but at a curt glare from Tyler, the young man just nodded and backed away.

When it was finally just the two of them standing in their corner at the top of the world, Tyler stared at her again, taking in each detail of her face. Even with the dirt smudge on her nose, she was beautiful. And she was his.

He just needed to convince her of it. He wanted her to know without a doubt that he loved her and would wait as long as it took for her to be able to love him in return.

He opened his mouth to say everything he needed to, but she lifted her fingers and touched his lips, halting his words and his thoughts.

Shoot. She didn't want him there, didn't want to hear him out.

He braced his shoulders. He'd come all this way, and

he had to at least say something. "Kinsey, I—"

She didn't let him finish and instead cupped her hand entirely over his mouth. "I'm sorry. I love you. And if you'll give me a second chance, I'll take it." The words were low and rushed, almost as if she'd rehearsed them and needed to say them just as rapidly as possible before she lost her nerve.

She stood watching him, obviously waiting for his reaction. With her hand over his mouth. Giving him no way to speak.

Her eyes were wide and filled with fear. Why? Because she was afraid he'd reject her? Surely she had to realize that his showing up here on the top of Mount Elbert was a pretty grand gesture, that he wouldn't have made the climb if he didn't love her.

Even so, she was waiting, her forehead furrowing.

Maybe he didn't have to speak. Maybe it was just time to show her that they would always have second chances, and third, and fourth, and as many as it took, because he was all in forever.

He lifted his hand to hers and flattened her cupped hand so that he could kiss her palm. He let his lips linger there for long seconds, not once breaking eye contact with her.

Her shoulders seemed to relax a little, but uncertainty still flitted through her eyes. "I was a coward, but I don't want to let my fears hold me back any longer."

Her words were far more than he'd expected, and they filled him with a happiness he hadn't thought he'd feel so quickly. But he should have guessed that with Kinsey, he'd fall again for her just as fast and furiously as he had from the start. Was this what he'd feel for the rest of his life with her? Was this what all his ancestors had felt too?

With fresh fire sparking along his nerves, he kissed her palm again.

Her wide eyes blazed to life with the heat he loved seeing there. Even so, she seemed to be banking the sparks, not quite ready to let them spread.

This time, he reached for her hip and drew her body against his, firmly and decisively. Then in the next move, he bent in and let her hand fall away so that he was kissing her mouth with just as much firmness and decisiveness.

He let his kiss tell her everything—that she was the one for him, the only woman he'd ever want, the love of his life.

As he took the kiss from zero to a hundred miles per hour in one second, she met him as she usually did, with the same fervor. He almost groaned with how much he loved her passion and her ability to meet him kiss for kiss without any hesitation and without any holding back.

Her hands wrapped around his neck, and she melded against him, as if she couldn't get close enough. He didn't hesitate to draw her in and fold her tighter.

He could keep on kissing her all day and all night and never grow tired of it, but at the sound of clapping, whistles, and catcalls, he pulled back. He was tempted to glare at the other hikers, but Kinsey took a step away from him, a smile lighting up her face.

She beamed at the others, then at Mitch, before turning her full smile upon him.

As she tilted her head and peered up at him, he was tempted to bend down and kiss her full on the lips again just as desperately, because he was so desperately in love with her that he wanted her to know it over and over for the rest of her life.

"So," she said, "does that kiss mean you accept my apology?"

"It means"—he couldn't stop from kissing her forehead—"that no apology is necessary."

"But I am sorry—"

He cut her off by kissing the tip of her nose. "I came up here because I couldn't go another day without letting you know that I'll always love you, that I'm fighting for us, and that I'll be waiting for you whenever you're ready."

She cocked her head, her smile still bright. "Ready for what?"

"Ready to be in a relationship with me."

"I'm ready, Tyler."

"But I don't want to rush you and end up pushing

you away. I already did that, and I want to be careful. After today, of course. I know this is pushy coming up here like this and interrupting your hike and interfering with your vacation."

"I'm done. I was talking with Mitch about leaving. After the hike, I wanted to call Kade and have him come pick me up so that I could talk to you."

"You did?" Tyler could feel a smile of his own working free.

"I realized I've let my fears keep me from climbing my difficult mountains for too long and I've been missing out on so much beauty." She glanced around at the view with awe before returning her gaze to him as if he was an even better view. "And now I want to move forward. With you."

He bent in and touched his lips to hers again, unable to stop himself, not caring that everyone else was still watching them. She was his. And he wanted the whole world to know.

More than that, he wanted to make sure she knew how much he loved her. He intended to make sure she knew it every day, every hour, and every minute for the rest of their lives.

25

"Happy birthday, dear Da-ad. Happy birthday to you."
The song rang out loudly in the July evening as the whole
family surrounded T.W. on the deck that overlooked the
ranch. It was a special birthday this year after his battle
with cancer, a milestone to reach his fifty-ninth year.

Kinsey stood beside Tyler, his arm wrapped around
her and drawing her to his side. She'd slipped her arm
around his waist too, loving being connected.

Emberly began cutting an enormous cake and passing
out pieces. Kade and Dustin sat on one side of the table,
sipping drinks. Wyatt leaned against Brock's chair and
stared with adoration at the uncle who *liked to sing and
play the guitar.*

The boy had been by Kinsey's side throughout most
of the family gathering, eager to talk to her and be with
her as he always was. Thankfully, he'd adjusted well to the
news that she and Tyler were dating. After Wyatt had

returned home from his trip to New York at the end of June, Tyler had sat down with the boy and told him everything, and Wyatt had been genuinely excited to find out his dad was in love with her.

Of course, Wyatt didn't understand all the implications of falling in love. But he'd apparently been able to see that his dad was happier, and he'd accepted Kinsey's presence in their lives as if it was natural and right for her to be there.

Kinsey had expected some pushback, maybe a little acting out, or even some questions. But clearly Tyler had done a good job of explaining what their relationship meant without harming Wyatt's connection with Stephanie.

It probably also helped that Wyatt had just spent time with Stephanie and had grasped in his own way that Stephanie would always be on the fringes of his life and never someone who loved him as fully and deeply as the rest of his family.

Whatever the case, Wyatt seemed happy to have Kinsey involved in his and Tyler's life. She'd grown to love the boy over the past weeks of spending time with both him and Tyler and doing all kinds of fun things together. The two had made sure she'd been able to experience everything the ranch had to offer, from white water rafting to the rifle range. She'd continued her riding lessons, and they'd even done a painting class.

Tyler leaned into her and pressed a kiss to her temple. "I love you, darlin'," he whispered.

She loved that he was so affectionate, as though he couldn't show her enough how much he cared about her. She peered up at him, relishing that this handsome man with his rugged and fierce looks belonged to her. "I love you too."

She reached up to steal a quick, sweet kiss from him. But of course, the moment their lips met, the usual sparks flared to life, and the kiss was neither quick nor sweet.

"Ah, c'mon, you two." Brock released an exasperated groan. "Is kissing all you do?"

With heat rushing to her cheeks, she tried to break free. But Tyler held her in place for a moment longer as if to show off for his brother. Or to prove to Brock that he would kiss his woman whenever and however he wanted.

When Tyler broke the kiss, he grinned at Brock. "And that's how it's done."

Brock chuckled. "You got real lucky with Kinsey. Don't know how you did it with as ugly as you are."

Kinsey had learned that the siblings teased each other all the time. Even though it made her miss Madison, she enjoyed the banter and the camaraderie and the love the McQuaids shared for each other.

Tyler smirked at Brock. "Not as ugly as you, that's for sure."

They were both ridiculously handsome, Brock maybe

even more so than Tyler, if that were even possible. Maybe it was Brock's crooked grin or his seductive eyes or the casual drawl of his words.

Whatever it was, women everywhere loved him and flocked toward him. Now that he'd broken up with his girlfriend, Ainsley Rose, he'd probably be swamped with interest.

He'd told his family about the breakup when he'd arrived, had called things off on a recent trip to visit Ainsley Rose. He didn't seem upset about it. According to Tyler, Brock was never in any relationship for too long before moving on.

T.W. was smiling at everyone and holding Leah on his lap, her arms wrapped around his neck. This week he'd been stronger and had more energy, which was why Kinsey had consented to having the birthday party outside on the deck.

As far as she could tell in the two months she'd lived at Healing Springs Ranch, he was winning the fight against cancer. He'd recovered quickly from his surgery for the obstruction and had gone through one round of chemotherapy, which had consisted of three weeks of treatments and a rest week.

Even though the trips to Colorado Springs were draining and the medicine took a toll, T.W. didn't complain. He was in good spirits, especially whenever his whole family was together. Like they had been for the

Fourth of July and now today for his birthday at the end of the month.

Kinsey was still his primary nurse, even though he technically didn't need a nurse any longer since he was medically stable. But T.W. insisted she stay for the duration of his rounds—four more—and the McQuaids insisted on continuing to pay for her.

But she'd told Tyler only yesterday that as soon as T.W. finished chemotherapy, she could no longer accept any pay for his care. Not only didn't he need her, but she and Tyler had begun making plans to build an Urgent Care Center in Healing Springs. They'd already looked at several vacant lots and had hired an architect to come up with a design.

She intended to head up the new medical facility and also planned to work there as a critical care nurse. The prospect excited her immensely, was the next chapter of her life, and would allow her to stay in the area to be with Tyler and Wyatt.

The trouble was that she needed to start looking for a place of her own to live. Even though she was still facing her fears and climbing the proverbial mountains in her life, the thought of signing a lease scared her. At times she still questioned if she'd been right to quit being a traveling nurse and put in her resignation with Premier.

Of course, Tyler had said he'd support whatever she chose to do, had told her they'd make a way to be together even if she wanted to continue working with Premier. He'd offered to travel with her for part of the time, and she'd discussed the option of taking shorter trips and assignments that wouldn't last as long.

In the end, though, she'd realized she needed to let go of the traveling for a while, if not permanently. Living in one place would be different and maybe even scary, but she wanted to take that next step.

Tyler had told her she could stay in her current room and remain at the main house, but she knew she had to go, had to take the next step in having her own apartment. Besides, it was also getting harder to keep her relationship with Tyler from combusting. Although they'd tried to curb their kissing so that they could work on building a friendship and a solid relationship, their attraction was strong. It was getting harder not to become carried away when they were alone, and she hoped that moving out would dampen the sparks a little.

"I've got the best woman in the world," Tyler said, dropping a kiss on Kinsey's head. "And I'm keeping her forever."

Brock's brow rose, and he shared a knowing look with Tyler. Then Brock ruffled Wyatt's hair. "Hey, kid. Can you go get my guitar for me? It's sitting in the front entryway."

"Sure, Uncle Brock." Wyatt bounded away eagerly.

"Think you want to keep me forever too?" Tyler

whispered, his tone suddenly intense.

They'd already had many conversations about the future, and Tyler had made it clear many times that she was the true love of his life, that he would never let her get away and would always fight for them.

He'd proven that already with a tenacity that had made her feel wanted and special. With how well he loved her, like she was a rare treasure that he revered, how could she not love him more in response? His tenderness and devotion were the same as T.W.'s for Leah, and such tenderness and devotion was irresistible.

Kinsey knew now why Leah adored T.W. in return. It was impossible not to flourish under such love.

She peered up at Tyler and smiled. "I'll never want another man ever again." It was the truth. She'd been given a rare gift in this McQuaid man. "And I want to keep you forever and ever and ever."

His expression relaxed. "Good."

Had he been worried? Why?

She started to formulate a question, but Wyatt was already stepping back onto the deck with Brock's guitar. She'd wait until later, when she and Tyler were alone, to ask him more about his worry, and she would assure him she loved him back.

Wyatt rushed over and gave the guitar to Brock.

"Thanks, kid." He fist-bumped Wyatt. Then he situated his guitar on his knee. "I've got a new song I'd like to sing tonight for you guys."

At the announcement, his family stopped their conversations and gave him their attention.

Sometimes she couldn't believe she was really interacting with Brock McQuaid. She tried not to act starstruck around him, but it was hard not to at moments like this when he sang for them—a private concert with a brand-new song that no one else had yet heard.

"I actually wrote this for Ty." Brock shared another glance with Tyler.

Tyler nodded, his dark eyes intense.

"He called me last week and asked if I could come up with something, and I said I'd do anything to help him win the woman he loves."

Kinsey's heart jumped ahead an extra beat. Tyler had asked Brock to write a song regarding her? She turned questioning eyes upon Tyler, but he didn't meet her gaze, was instead focused on his brother.

Brock's rugged and gritty voice began the song in typical country music style, with a story about a lonely man living in misery, drowning his sorrows with no hope for the tomorrows.

"But then I met you-ou-ou," Brock sang to an achingly sweet tune. "And I knew it was true-ue-ue. When you find the one you're looking for, there's nothing else that matters more, than making her your one and only. Your one and only."

Tyler squeezed her tighter to his side, his muscular arm hard and possessive, telling her that every word of the song was resonating from his heart.

Tears sprang to her eyes. She didn't deserve a man so sweet and devoted, but she intended to love him back with everything inside her.

"We're gonna chase after forever." Brock's voice carried through the evening air. "And we're gonna do it together. No matter if the spurs kick us down, the sparks of our love will abound."

Brock hummed for a moment and gave a nod to Tyler.

He pulled away from her.

As always, she was reluctant to let go of him. There was nowhere else she'd rather be than right by his side at all times. And she knew he felt the same…not only because he always told her that, but because he held her whenever he had the chance.

Digging in his pocket, he fidgeted for a moment. Before she knew what was happening, he lowered himself to one knee in front of her and held up a small velvet box.

It was open. And nestled inside was a diamond ring.

Her heartbeat tripped and then came to an abrupt halt. Was this what she thought it was?

Her gaze flew to Tyler's, and excitement raced through her body.

Love and assurance radiated from his eyes. His

handsome face held a firmness and steadiness and determination that told her this was exactly what he wanted...*she* was exactly who he wanted. And that he wouldn't be swayed.

"Kinsey, you're the one I'm looking for, and now there's nothing else that matters more, than making you my one and only." Tyler repeated the words from Brock's song, and she knew it would be their song forever. "You'll make me the happiest man if you agree to become my wife."

She blinked back the swift tears of happiness that burned in her eyes. "Yes." She could barely get the word out past her constricted throat.

A shimmer misted his eyes too. Then he removed the ring from the box and slipped it on her finger.

Everyone in the family started whooping and hollering while Brock sang the chorus again: "But then I met you-ou-ou. And I knew it was true-ue-ue."

With the ring firmly in place, she held out her hand. It was stunning on her finger with the evening sunlight glinting on the diamond. Awe spread through her. She was engaged to the man she loved more than life. And now she'd get to spend forever with him.

Tyler rose and reached for her. As he pulled her close, he dipped down and meshed his lips with hers in one of his hungry and powerful kisses.

The words of their song surrounded them in an

achingly sweet melody: "When you find the one you're looking for, there's nothing else that matters more, than making her your one and only. Your one and only."

Author's Note

Hi, friends! I hope you enjoyed this new venture of mine into writing a contemporary romance series! It was very fun for me to let loose a little bit and write outside the stricter historical romance parameters that I'm used to, especially with language and style.

Currently I have six books planned in the McQuaid Legacy series. But already I can see more stories formulating for minor characters like Nettie, the single mom who seems like she needs a happily-ever-after.

Next up, though, is Brock McQuaid. The country music star can't seem to make relationships work, and with his most recent breakup, he's garnering some bad publicity. People are beginning to doubt that the man who sings about love really knows what love is all about. What lengths will Brock go to in order to save his career and prove that he can practice what he preaches?

I hope you'll enjoy Brock's venture into learning about love and what it takes to have a truly meaningful relationship.

Until then…why not take a trip through time and see how the whole McQuaid family and the legacy of love started? My sweet historical romance series, The Colorado Cowboys, is set in the 1860s and chronicles the original Wyatt McQuaid settling on the land that eventually becomes Healing Springs Ranch. Join him and his siblings as they find love in the high country of Colorado. (I've included the first two chapters of *A Cowboy for Keeps* in the back of this book so that you can get a taste of the original Wyatt's story!)

As always, I love hearing from YOU! If you haven't yet joined my Facebook Reader Room, what are you waiting for!? It's a great place to keep up to date on all my book releases and book news, as well as a fun place to connect with other readers and me.

Until next time…

Find out where it all began in this heart-warming historical romance series! Join the McQuaid family as they seek new opportunities and find love in the wild and unsettled land of Colorado in the 1860s.

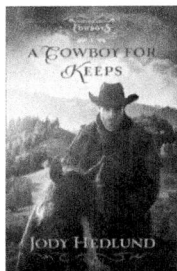

A Cowboy for Keeps

Wyatt McQuaid is struggling to get his new ranch up and running and is in town to purchase cattle when the mayor proposes the most unlikely of bargains. He'll invest in a herd of cattle for Wyatt's ranch if Wyatt agrees to help the town become more respectable by marrying and starting a family. And the mayor has just the candidate in mind for Wyatt to marry.

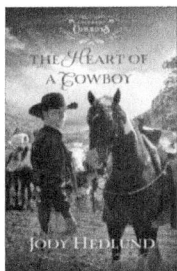

The Heart of a Cowboy

After watching his ma suffer and die in childbirth, Flynn McQuaid has sworn off women and marriage forever. Headed west to start a new life, he has his hands full not only taking care of his younger siblings but also delivering cattle to his older brother. He doesn't need more complications in falling for a woman he's determined not to love.

To Tame a Cowboy

Brody McQuaid is a broken man, and he knows it. While his body survived the war, his soul did not. Besides loving his little niece, his only sense of purpose comes from saving the wild horses that roam South Park. When the new veterinarian on the ranch turns her gentle healing touch on him, he's not sure that he's ready to tame his fears.

Falling for the Cowgirl

As the only girl in her family, and with four older brothers, Ivy McQuaid can rope and ride with the roughest of ranchers. She's ready to have what she's always longed for—a home of her own. She's set her heart on a parcel of land south of Fairplay and is saving for it with her winnings from the cowhand competitions she sneaks into. But her dream is put in jeopardy when the man she once loved reappears in her life.

Last Chance Cowboy

The repentant prodigal Dylan McQuaid is finally back in Fairplay. As sheriff, he's doing his best to prove to the town he's a changed man and worthy of their trust. When a woman shows up with an infant son he didn't know he had, Dylan is left with only complicated choices on what to do next.

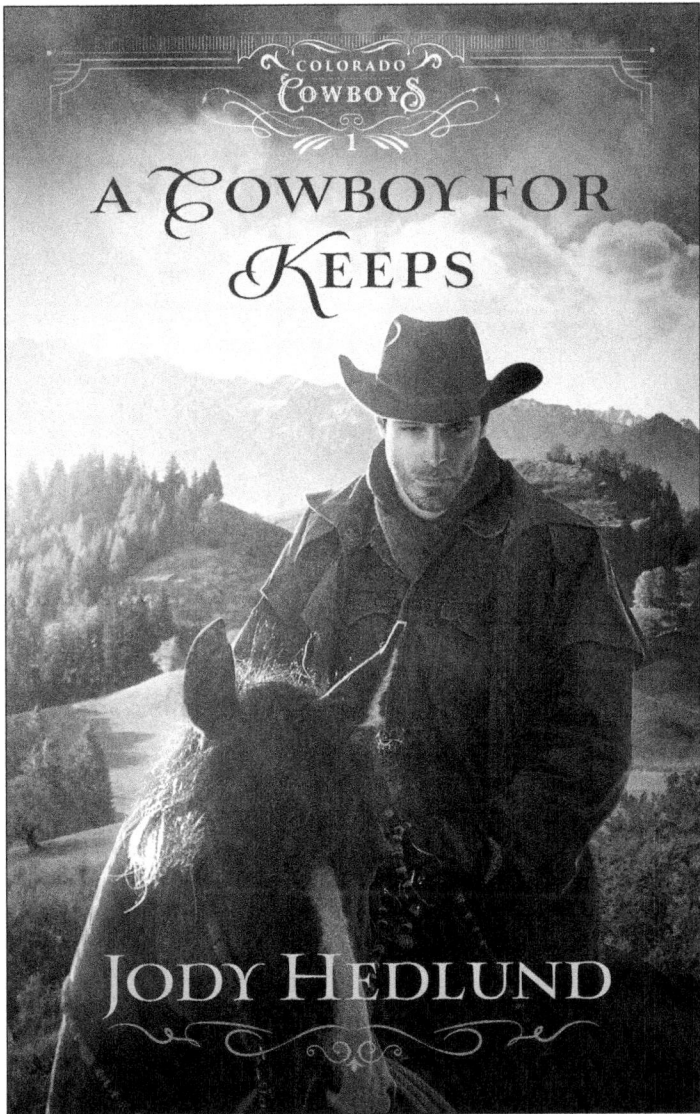

A COWBOY FOR KEEPS

JODY HEDLUND

COLORADO
COWBOYS
1

A COWBOY FOR KEEPS

JODY HEDLUND

BETHANYHOUSE
a division of Baker Publishing Group
Minneapolis, Minnesota

CHAPTER

1

Colorado Territory
August 1862

"Stop or we'll shoot!" A dozen feet up Kenosha Pass, three robbers with flour sacks over their heads blocked the way, their revolvers outstretched.

Walking alongside the stagecoach, Greta Nilsson didn't have to be told twice. She froze—all except her pulse, which sped to a thundering gallop.

Next to her, the Concord jerked to a halt.

"Come out and put your hands up where we can see 'em," called the lanky robber at the center, peering through unevenly cut holes in his mask.

Greta raised her gloved hands and hoped they weren't trembling. Likewise, the two gentlemen hiking near her wasted no time in obeying.

Before she'd left Illinois, everyone had warned her of the trouble she might encounter on the route to the west, including the growing problem of stagecoach robberies. Over the past eight weeks of traveling, she'd braced herself for the possibility, had mentally rehearsed such an encounter and what she'd do.

But today, on the last day of the journey, she'd finally allowed herself to relax and believe that for once things might work out in her favor, that she hadn't made a big mistake in moving to Colorado.

Apparently, she'd assumed too much too soon.

At the rear of the stagecoach, several men had been pushing it the last distance to the top of the pass, and they now eased out into the open, their arms up. The driver sitting on his bench atop the stagecoach set the brake, then released the reins controlling the two teams of horses that had been straining to pull them up the mountain. He, too, cautiously lifted his hands.

She guessed, like her, the other passengers were well aware of the tales of murder and mayhem along the wilderness trails. And they weren't taking any chances either.

At least Astrid was inside the coach. After trekking uphill for the first hour, the little girl's poor lungs hadn't been able to handle the exertion. As much as Astrid had loathed returning to the bumpy conveyance, she'd been able to have a seat to herself since everyone else had gotten out to lighten the load.

Last time Greta had peeked through the open

windows, her sister had been sprawled out asleep, and now Greta prayed the precocious child would stay that way.

The middle robber inched toward them, his revolver swinging in a wide arc. His leathery hands and dirt-encrusted fingernails contrasted with the ivory handle of his revolver. "Nobody move."

Morning sunlight filtered through the aspens, their white bark and green-gold leaves making the trail feel more open and airy than other parts of the mountainous road. A cool, dry breeze rattled the leaves, swishing like ladies' skirts brushing against grass.

Just minutes ago, Greta had been marveling at how different the dry and cooler climate was from northern Illinois where oppressive humidity plagued the summers and made every chore feel like a burden. What she wouldn't give at this moment to be back there shucking corn or snapping beans, even if she was dripping with perspiration.

"Anyone left inside?" one of the other robbers asked.

"No," Greta said quickly. "Everyone's out."

Just then the stagecoach door inched open.

The lanky robber with the uneven eye slits swung his revolver toward the door and clicked the hammer.

"No!" Greta threw herself between the robber and the stagecoach, shoving against Astrid's strong push.

A short distance away beyond the trees, the

mountainside overlooked the sprawling grasslands of South Park, nestled between the Front Range in the east and the Mosquito Range in the west. Their destination was within eyesight. If only it was also within shouting distance so they could call for help.

The bandit shifted the barrel's aim to Greta, his arm stiff, his fingers taut. "Woman, unless you want to find yourself eating a bullet, you'd best step aside and let that person out."

Inside, Astrid cried out in protest and once again attempted to open the door. But Greta flattened the full length of her body against it.

"Move on outta the way, woman," the robber said, louder and more irritably.

"It's her little sister." One of the other passengers moved to stand beside Greta, a middle-aged man who'd introduced himself as Landry Steele yesterday morning when they boarded the stagecoach in Denver. He'd spent the majority of the journey conversing with the other gentlemen. However, during the few brief interactions she'd had with him, he'd always been considerate.

"The girl is ill and is of no concern to you." Beneath the brim of Mr. Landry's bowler, he shot Greta an apologetic look, as though realizing she'd wanted to keep Astrid hidden away and out of the conflict.

"That so?" The gunman's revolver didn't waver. "If she's of no concern, then let her on out."

Greta pressed against the door harder. She hadn't brought Astrid all this distance to have her die at the hand of a robber. "She's only eight years old—"

"I'm nine," came Astrid's indignant voice.

"Allow her to come out," Mr. Landry said with a quiet urgency. "You don't want her to end up an orphan, do you?"

Astrid an orphan? Never in Greta's plans had she counted on dying before Astrid. The truth was, Astrid's days were numbered, and Greta hoped to lengthen and make them as pain-free as possible. But she couldn't do that if she let the robber kill her.

Swallowing hard, Greta stepped away from the stagecoach. The door flew open with a bang, and Astrid tumbled out. She landed with an *oomph* onto the grassy road but then bounded up as nimbly as a barn cat. Though the consumption had emaciated the girl so that she was thin and petite for her age, somehow she still retained a fresh and vibrant spirit that made up for her physical frailty.

Her big silver blue eyes, so much like Greta's, took in the scene—the robbers, their guns, and all the passengers standing motionless with hands in the air. Astrid's hair was also the same color as Greta's, a golden brown now sun-streaked from so many days of neglecting her bonnet. Astrid had refused to allow Greta to plait her hair when they'd arisen at half past four in the morning for a hasty departure from the stagecoach station, and now it hung in tangled waves.

Even so, Astrid was the picture of perfection. She had dainty porcelain but beautiful features that drew attention everywhere she went. Greta had never considered herself to be a beauty, not like some of the other young women back home and certainly not like Astrid.

But too many people to recount during the journey west had exclaimed how much she and Astrid looked alike. The admiring glances and flattery had been strange but not unwelcome. At times, she wondered if maybe she was prettier than she'd realized, if maybe she'd been hasty in accepting the first mail-order bride proposal that came along.

Astrid took a step in the direction of the closest robber. "Why are you wearing a sack over your head?"

"Astrid, come here this instant," Greta whispered in her sternest tone.

The thief's gaze darted to the passengers and back to Astrid, revealing a crooked, lazy eye that didn't focus. "It's what robbers do, kid."

"W-e-l-l." Astrid drew the word out and cocked her head. "It makes you look kinda silly, like a scarecrow."

Greta lunged for Astrid, but the girl dodged away and skipped toward the robber.

His gun wavered, as though he was considering turning the weapon on Astrid.

"Astrid!" Horror rose in Greta's throat, threatening to strangle her. "Don't you dare go a step closer."

Astrid halted and held out her hand. "Here's some money, Mister. It's mine, but you can have it since you need it more than me."

The man's lazy eye shifted to Astrid again. "Drop it on the ground."

Astrid released a crumpled wad and a few coins. They bounced in the grass near the robber's feet. "My sister has more—"

"No!" Greta couldn't let these bandits discover her secret stash since she'd taken pains to sew the money into the lining of her coat after the passengers had been warned not to carry valuables.

It was her jam money. Her earnings from picking and preserving the wild berries that grew on the farm. The accumulation of two years of working every spare minute.

Astrid turned her pretty eyes upon Greta. "They have to wear flour sacks instead of hats. Guess that means they need the money more than we do. Right, Mister?"

"Right, kid." This time the robber's voice hinted at amusement.

The thieves made quick work at emptying the locked box next to the driver and then divested each of the passengers of anything of value. Within a few minutes they ran off into the woods with their loot.

Greta stood with the others, surveying their

belongings strewn over the grass surrounding the stagecoach. Astrid had lost interest in the robbers and was intent on picking a bouquet of wildflowers.

"We got lucky." The driver broke the silence, his voice shaky as he closed the now-empty box next to him. "Last time the Crooked-Eye Gang struck, they killed three men—"

Mr. Steele cut off the driver with a glare and a curt nod toward Astrid.

The driver clamped his mouth closed, and everyone set to work repacking their bags and trunks.

Greta fingered the frayed coat hem. Although Phineas Hallock, her intended, had assured her he had plenty of money since he was part owner of a gold mine, she couldn't keep dismay from weighing upon her.

She'd corresponded with Phineas by letter on several occasions last year, and she sensed in him genuine kindness, especially since he'd so readily agreed to take care of Astrid. He also made all the arrangements for the trip, including paying for their fare.

Though the small daguerreotype he'd sent in his last letter the previous summer had shown him to be a plain-looking and somewhat older man, his face held a look of integrity as well as honesty. Maybe he wasn't handsome or young, but that didn't matter. What she needed was a husband who was reliable, dependable, and able to provide for her and Astrid.

Besides, after making up her mind, Greta had wanted to move as quickly as possible to get Astrid to the healing air of the Rockies. Why waste time corresponding with other men when Phineas had been so eager and ready to help her?

Maybe she'd acted rashly. But what was done, was done. She was on her way to marry Phineas. She would, in fact, wed him by the day's end.

Still, she blinked back tears. All of her savings were gone. If only Astrid knew how to obey better. . . . If only the little girl had a real mother and father to raise her. . . . Instead, she was stuck with a mere half sister who clearly didn't know how to keep her in line. . . .

Greta sat back on her heels and watched the young girl with a mixture of frustration and helplessness.

"Don't be too hard on her." Mr. Steele bent next to Greta and retrieved a shiny leather shoe.

"She's a handful."

"She saved some of us from meeting our Maker today."

"She did?"

The gentleman removed his bowler and smoothed back his dark hair, which had hints of gray at his temples and streaking his long sideburns and mustache. "The gang leader liked her and showed mercy on us as a result."

Mercy? Each of the passengers had lost everything of value. But she supposed that was better than losing their lives.

"I have a son about Astrid's age." Mr. Steele replaced his hat, watching Astrid wistfully.

"You must be looking forward to seeing him when we arrive in Fairplay."

He focused on the child a moment longer, his expression filled with sadness. "Unfortunately, I won't be seeing him anytime soon. He lives in New York with his mother."

"I'm sorry." Greta didn't know what else to say.

Mr. Steele shook his head, as if by doing so he could shake away his morose thoughts. "Tell me again why you're moving to Fairplay."

Greta hadn't told him anything yet, since he hadn't asked. But she wouldn't be so impolite as to say so. Instead, she gave him the rehearsed line she'd spouted to everyone else who'd wanted to know. "My fiancé lives in Fairplay, and I'm traveling there to marry him."

"Your fiancé? Is that so?" Mr. Steele's eyes lit with interest. "May I ask who the lucky fellow is? I'm mayor and have gotten to know many men in the area."

All the misgivings she'd had since agreeing to marry Phineas soared. What if she'd made a mistake in coming west and agreeing to marry a stranger? What if he wasn't who he had claimed to be? What if he mistreated Astrid?

Just as quickly as the doubts assailed her, she tossed them aside. If Phineas wasn't the man he'd portrayed in his letters, then she'd have no obligation to stay with him.

In fact, perhaps Mr. Steele would be able to advise her regarding the true nature of Phineas's character. Then if her fiancé had any glaring faults, she'd be well aware of them before arriving in Fairplay.

She cast a sideways glance at the other passengers, who were in the finishing stages of stowing their belongings and were thankfully heedless of the conversation. "I haven't actually met my intended."

Mr. Steele, in the process of picking up another shoe, paused.

"We've written to each other."

He straightened and gave her his full attention. "You wouldn't happen to be Phineas Hallock's mail-order bride, would you?"

Something in his tone made the skin at the back of her neck prickle with unease. "Yes, Mr. Hallock is my fiancé. Do you know him?"

The gentleman shook his head, his features creasing. "I knew him well. He was a good man."

Her heart began to patter fast and hard. "Knew?"

"I'm sorry, Miss Nilsson. Phineas Hallock is dead."

"The mine owner Phineas Hallock, originally from Connecticut?"

"Yes, he left for California last autumn. Said he was traveling there to purchase supplies for his new bride and that he planned to be back by late spring. When the thawing came and he didn't return, we all thought he was delayed. Until a body was discovered on Hoosier Pass."

"His body?"

"As far as we can tell, after so many months of being exposed to the elements. . . ."

She stared at Mr. Steele, but somehow he faded from her vision. All she could see was the black-and-white photograph of Phineas.

In his last letter, he'd mentioned his trip to California and his excitement over picking out additional furniture and items for their home. He expressed his desire to have the newly built house well-stocked and ready for her arrival. She hadn't heard from him since and assumed he hadn't had the opportunity to send further correspondence. Even if he had, mail delivery via the Pony Express and stagecoach wasn't reliable. Letters were sometimes lost or stolen.

Besides, she'd been busy preparing for the trip, sewing clothes for Astrid and her, packing their belongings, and saying good-byes. She'd never in her wildest imagination believed Phineas Hallock hadn't written again because he was dead.

He was dead.

She swayed, her vision growing fuzzy.

Mr. Steele's grip on her elbow steadied her. "I'm truly sorry, Miss Nilsson."

With a deep breath, she tried to bring the world back into focus. The sunlight streaming through the aspen branches above splashed across her face as though to wake her from a nightmare.

The man she'd come west to marry was dead. Every penny of her savings had just been stolen. What would she do now? How could she, a lone woman with a sick child, survive in the wilderness knowing no one and having nothing?

CHAPTER

2

The cold barrel of a revolver jammed into the back of Wyatt McQuaid's neck and stopped him short in the middle of Fairplay's dusty Main Street.

"Quit stealing my business." The voice—and the sour body odor—behind Wyatt belonged to only one man: Roper Brawley.

"I ain't stealing your business—"

"Jansen's steers were mine." Brawley dug the steel into Wyatt's neck, bumping and loosening his hat so it tumbled to the street.

Against the black felt, the chalky line from dried sweat was all too visible and encrusted along the brim with dust, grease, and mud spots. The center was dented where a heifer had recently trampled it. And the hatband of braided horsehair hung loose.

Even if his hat wasn't pretty, it was still his pride and

joy. And he wouldn't stand for anyone knocking it from his head.

With a jab backward, Wyatt elbowed Brawley's stomach, forcing the man to double over. With the pressure gone, Wyatt spun, latched on to Brawley's gun arm, and slammed it down hard against his knee, giving Brawley little choice but to release the revolver.

The weapon flew several feet, landing in the gravel, far enough away that Brawley couldn't easily reach it.

"This here is a free country." Wyatt swiped up his hat and situated it on his head. Although the sun was on its evening hike down to Sheep and Horseshoe Mountains, the rays were still strong and hot. "The miners can sell their oxen to anyone in the blazes they want to."

Nursing his stomach, Brawley straightened. A black patch covered a missing eye but couldn't hide the thin, white scars scattered across his cheek—wounds he'd gotten fighting Indians. "Me and my men were here in South Park first."

That was debatable. Wyatt had arrived in the summer of sixty and tried gold mining like thousands of other prospectors. After scraping by and managing to pan only enough nuggets and gold dust to fill his pockets, he'd tried his luck at something different—ranching.

With the passing of the Homestead Act earlier in the year, he'd been one of the first to file an application and pay the registration fee at the land office in Denver. He'd gotten himself one hundred sixty acres allowed under President Lincoln's new legislation fair and square.

His pasturelands spread out to the southeast of Fairplay. Wyatt had spent the spring and summer laboring from sunup to sundown, building a house and a barn on his claim. He and Judd had buckled down and made the place livable for both man and beast. And over recent weeks, he'd started adding more steers to his small herd.

And now, Roper Brawley was determined to keep him from succeeding.

Brawley crossed his arms and nodded at several cowhands loitering outside Cabinet Billiard Hall. At their boss's signal, they sauntered toward Wyatt, their spurs jangling, their hands resting on the handles of their six-shooters tucked into their holsters.

Wyatt made eye contact with Judd, who stood next to the livery guarding the two bone-thin steers Wyatt had just purchased. The white-haired man limped forward too. He didn't reach for his Colts—didn't have to. Judd was the fastest gunslinger in the Rockies. He could shoot iron quicker than the twitch of a cow's tail.

Fortunately, Brawley and his men knew it. They stopped a dozen paces away, feet spread, hands at the ready.

Brawley spit a stream of tobacco into the street, then wiped his sleeve across his mouth. "This place ain't big enough for the two of us, McQuaid."

"If that's the way you feel, then I guess you oughta be moving on."

"You're the one needing to move on." Brawley's bottom lip rounded out from the chew stuffed inside, and his thin, scraggly beard and mustache were stained with the juice. Brawley probably wasn't much older than Wyatt's own twenty-three years, but his lean, leathery face and somber eyes spoke of hardships that had aged him too soon.

"Come on now, Brawley." Wyatt attempted to dredge up some empathy for the man. After all, he knew a bit about hardships himself. "This land here in South Park can handle more than one ranch. Let's aim to live in peace—"

"Peace?" Brawley scoffed. "You buying up all the cattle and leaving me with none ain't aiming for peace."

Wyatt almost snorted but held himself back. Brawley had things backward. He was the one buying up the weak and worn out oxen as rapidly as the miners and teamsters came over the passes.

The rumbling of wheels and the pounding of hooves from the northeast end of town cut off their discussion. *Discussion* was too kind a word for Brawley's attempt to intimidate Wyatt into leaving. It wasn't the first time the rancher had made threats, and it probably wouldn't be the last.

As the stagecoach rolled closer, the clatter and dust rose higher. Brawley bent and retrieved his revolver and then headed toward his men. Across the street, Judd watched with unswerving intensity, his bushy white eyebrows narrowed and his white mustache pursed until the men disappeared into the billiard hall. Once gone, Judd tipped the brim of his hat at Wyatt before he shuffled back toward the newly purchased steers.

Wyatt rolled his shoulders and tried to release the tension. At the rate he was going, he'd never make enough profit to send for his ma and siblings. Even if he could help his family with the costs of traveling to Colorado, how would he support them once they arrived?

What he needed to do was purchase a herd of purebred Shorthorns from the breeder he'd met in Missouri during his days transporting livestock for Russell, Major & Waddell. Beeves like that would thrive on the buffalograss, wheat grass, and moss sage.

He peered beyond the buildings that lined the street to the grassy plains that spread out to the distant Tarryall Mountain range in the east. Since the grass was endless and free, he'd have no trouble fattening up the cattle for butchering. The miners always had a hankering for beef, tiring easily of the fish they caught in local streams or the canned goods they bought for exorbitant prices.

In fact, if Wyatt could purchase a big enough herd of Shorthorns and start his own breeding, he'd be able to send a stream of beef to the markets in the east. Eventually, he might make enough from sales to buy up more of the surrounding land and expand his ranch.

The trouble was, he didn't have a tail feather left, not after pouring every penny of his savings into the start-up costs of his place. He could hardly afford the worn-out oxen that newcomers were practically giving away. Besides, he couldn't rely on that supply forever, especially with Brawley's bristles rising every time Wyatt made a purchase.

As the stage rolled to a jerking halt in front of the Fairplay Hotel, Wyatt expelled a pent-up breath. What he needed was an investor, a partner who'd be willing to help him build up his herd.

The gold mines in the mountains surrounding South Park had made millionaires out of numerous men. Would any of them be willing to invest in his ranch?

Wyatt scanned the buildings lining Fairplay, most having the typical false storefronts that made the businesses appear bigger and more significant to draw men in. Set at the center of the flat grasslands along the intersection of Beaver Creek and the South Platte, Fairplay had earned its name from its first prospectors who'd vowed that their mining camp would be different from the others in the area, that they'd operate with integrity and fairness.

Although the town had its share of taverns and dance

halls, it was a shade tamer than some of the other colorful mining towns that had sprung up in the area, towns like Buckskin Joe and Tarryall.

Of all the mining towns Wyatt had lived in and visited, he liked Fairplay best, mainly because he liked and respected the men who ran it.

Men like Landry Steele . . .

Steele stepped down from the stagecoach wearing his usual dark suit coat, vest, and matching trousers. He turned around and offered his hand to a woman in the stagecoach door.

The woman accepted the help descending. The brim of her bonnet hid her face, but from the litheness of her movements and the womanliness of her form, she was awful young to be Steele's wife. In the blue dress, the woman was also too plainly dressed to be Steele's fancy eastern wife. Besides, Steele had yammered on more than once about his wife refusing to live in the Wild West.

As the woman planted both feet on the ground, Steele reached up to the doorway again and, this time, offered his hand to a little girl.

Wyatt couldn't contain his surprise and released a low whistle. Maybe Steele's wife had decided to come west with their child after all, although hadn't Steele talked about a son, not a daughter?

The girl bounded down, her bonnet pushed back, revealing long, loose hair the color of a newborn fawn.

Petite and pretty, the child smiled her thanks to Steele before skipping away.

"Astrid, stay close." The woman spun after the child and revealed her face. Her hair was the same light brown as the child's, and her features were just as pretty but fuller and slightly rounder.

Astrid didn't heed her mother and frisked away from the stagecoach in the direction of Simpkin's General Store.

"Astrid, please." The woman grabbed a fistful of her skirt and picked up her pace, then cast a glance over her shoulder at Steele.

Steele smiled and waved her on. "Go and explore. You know where to find me."

She nodded, her expression emanating gratefulness, before she hustled after her child.

Stroking his mustache, Steele watched the young woman until she disappeared into the store behind the little girl.

Wyatt needed to stop staring, but his curiosity got the better of him. If this woman wasn't Steele's wife, then who was she? Couldn't be his mistress. Steele had never struck Wyatt as the type of man who'd cheat on his wife, no matter how much he had a hankering for a woman.

As if sensing the scrutiny, Steele's gaze swung to Wyatt, where he still stood in the middle of the road. Steele touched the brim of his bowler in greeting.

Wyatt repeated the action.

"Don't look at me like that McQuaid," Steele called.

"Like what?" Blast it all. Why hadn't he walked away before Steele had caught him staring?

"Like I'm doing something I shouldn't be."

"She ain't your wife, is she?"

"No, of course not." Steele huffed.

"I took you for a God-fearing man who took his marriage vows seriously."

"And I am."

"Then what are you doing with a pretty lady like that?" Wyatt glanced at the dusty window of the general store but couldn't see inside past the grime to the woman in question.

Steele pressed his lips together and crossed toward him. "Do you think she's pretty?"

Wyatt hadn't seen her long, but it had been enough to know she was a real beauty. "A man'd have to be blind not to think so."

Steele halted in front of him. The dust from the journey lightened the black of his suit coat to a charcoal gray. "Good. Then I want you to marry her."

GET YOUR COPY OF
A COWBOY FOR KEEPS NOW!!

A Cowboy for Keeps – Jody Hedlund
Bethany House, a division of Baker Publishing Group ©2021.

Jody Hedlund is the bestselling author of more than sixty novels and is the winner of numerous awards. Jody lives in Michigan with her husband, busy family, and five spoiled cats. She writes sweet romances with plenty of sizzle.

A complete list of my novels can be found at jody hedlund.com.

Would you like to know when my next book is available? You can sign up for my newsletter, become my friend on Goodreads, like me on Facebook, or follow me on Instagram.

Newsletter: jodyhedlund.com

Facebook: AuthorJodyHedlund

Instagram: @JodyHedlund

Printed in Dunstable, United Kingdom